What the critics are saying...

ജ

Winner of the Most Humorous category in the 2006 Anne-Bonney Readers' Choice Award contest

"This book, Hocus Pocus, is a sexy magical treat!" ~ *Molly O'Keefe, Harlequin Author*

5 angels "A brilliant, comedic romance that had me laughing intensely throughout. Hocus Pocus is surely one you will want to read again and again." ~ *Fallen Angels Reviews*

5 hearts "This reviewer absolutely loved this story. The reader will be hooked by the very first paragraph and will be taken on a roller coaster ride and will not want to be interrupted until the last word. Put up a big 'Do Not Disturb' sign before starting this book." ~ *Love Romance Reviews*

5 kisses "Teresa has a definite talent for writing comedy. With witty dialogue and snappy scenes, I couldn't put the book down." ~ *Romance Divas*

Teresa Roblin

Hocus Pocus

Cerridwen Press

A Cerridwen Press Publication

www.cerridwenpress.com

Hocus Pocus

ISBN 9781419955525
Edited by Kelli Kwiatkowski
Cover art by Niki Browning

Electronic book Publication December 2005
Trade paperback Publication January 2007

Cerridwen Press is an imprint of Ellora's Cave Publishing, Inc.®

About the Author

&

"Teresa has a tendency to daydream in class. She should pay more attention." That's what one of my elementary teachers wrote on my report card. I'm an adult now and I haven't changed a bit.

In 2000, I started writing my first book, Hocus Pocus, and within seven months it was completed. My second book, Now You See It…, was a year later. Naïve daydreamer that I am, I thought this is it, I'm going to get published. Optimistic, I entered my first book in a contest and placed last in the paranormal category.

So what did I do? I joined RWA, my local chapter, took writing courses, on-line workshops, talked to other writers and joined a critique group. I meant business and nothing and no one was holding me back from my dreams. By 2004, I was finally placing second and third in contests.

Now, everyone can read my books and share in my daydreams and understand why I usually walk around with a grin on my face.

Teresa welcomes comments from readers. You can find her website and email address on her author bio page at www.ellorascave.com

Trademarks Acknowledgment

The author acknowledges the trademarked status and trademark owners of the following wordmarks mentioned in this work of fiction:

Addams Family: Colyton, Barbara

Dolce & Gabbano: Gado S.A.R.L. Corporation

Foosball: Pro Sport Foosball Inc.

Honda Civic: Honda Motor Co.

Jaguar: Jaguar Cars Limited Corporation

Polo: PRL USA Holdings, Inc.

The Sopranos: Time Warner Entertainment Company

Styrofoam: Dow Chemical Company

Tiffany: Tiffany (NJ) Inc.

Walkman: Sony Kabushiki Kaisha TA Sony Corporation

HOCUS POCUS

&

Dedication

∽

To my husband and sons.
For believing in me and helping me live my dreams.
To my critique group - Mary, Maureen, Michele, Molly,
Sinead and Susan
Without you I wouldn't have got this far.

Chapter One

ഔ

Amanda confidently breezed off the elevator, her shoulders back, displaying a voluptuous hourglass figure encased in a soft cream dress that caressed her shape and fell above her knees. With a French-manicured finger, she wrapped a stray auburn curl behind her ear and felt her hair bounce against her shoulders with each self-assured step.

Passing the receptionists, Cindy and Misty, Amanda graced them with a quick smile and a brisk, "Good morning."

They returned her greeting with open smiles. "Good morning, Miss Santorelli." Their salutations followed her into her office.

Amanda found Mark, her boss, poised at the edge of her desk, a rose in hand. The way he greeted her every morning.

"Good morning," Amanda said in a low, husky voice. She was drawn into Mark's embrace as he gave her a light kiss to start the day.

"Hello, beautiful," Mark replied.

A man's shoulder bumped Amanda, jostling her out of her daydream. People hurried past, totally oblivious to her.

"Hey lady," a gruff voice snapped at Amanda, as several curious pairs of eyes turned to critically inspect her from inside the waiting elevator. "Move it, sugar, we haven't got all day."

Mortified, Amanda dashed onto the crowded lift, sucking in her breath as the mirrored doors closed in her face. Her cheeks heated at the sound of the passengers' snickers.

Inhaling deeply to calm her nerves, she recognized Mark Abbott's spicy cologne. Peeking to her left, Amanda found her boss two people over, leaning against the elevator wall, reading a folded newspaper. He hadn't even noticed her grand entrance.

Amanda's eyes traveled upward, past his muscular chest covered in a silver-gray silk shirt, over a familiar gray and red striped tie, paused to peek at the chiseled cleft in his chin and stopped at his clear blue eyes, which continued to scan the newspaper articles.

Looking around, Amanda caught the bored attention of some passengers. "Sorry," she whispered. She didn't dare glance at the mirrored doors for fear someone would still be staring at her. She just wanted to blend into the crowd and pretend her impressive entrance had never happened.

When the elevator doors opened to the third floor, several passengers got off and Peter, from Security, entered. He happened to be married to Stephanie, one of her sweetest cousins. Amanda tilted her head to look into his face. She enjoyed his blond hair, laughing brown eyes and harmless teasing.

"Hey there, gorgeous." Peter turned to face the elevator doors and raised his voice to ask, "So, is that boss of yours working you too hard?"

Blushing, Amanda pushed her gold-framed glasses up higher on the bridge of her nose. "No, he's not," she said, glancing toward Mark Abbott, who was frowning at Peter. From his confused expression, it was obvious that he wasn't sure to whom Peter had been speaking. Was she that invisible?

Amanda watched the two men nod at each other before Mark finally turned to her. "Good morning, Amanda, I hadn't seen you there." Mark smiled to the gentleman in front of him. "Excuse me, please." The passenger moved aside and Mark squeezed in next to her.

With a brief smile, Mark began asking Peter questions about the security at one of their company's job sites.

Again, dismissed and forgotten.

Sandwiched between two giants, Amanda followed their conversation and ended up feeling like she was watching a tennis match. Back and forth. Back and forth. Glancing at the rising floor numbers, Amanda wished the elevator would hurry so she could leave her embarrassment, and the feeling of being insignificant, behind.

The doors opened on the tenth floor, letting more passengers off. Only two floors left. When the elevator started again, Mark's arm brushed against hers. That light innocent touch sent Amanda's heart pounding, while Mark seemingly remained unaffected as he continued talking to Peter.

Amanda heard an annoyed "Hmm," from the back of the car. With a quick peek in the mirror, she spotted Agnes. Each time Amanda had the misfortune of passing her, Agnes would mumble or give her sour looks.

Ever since Amanda had competed for—and won—the position of Assistant to the CEO, the woman had held a grudge against her. Agnes had moved on to another company in the building, yet each time she saw Amanda she gave her a hard time.

Amanda inhaled a fortifying breath and slowly exhaled. *One of these days I'm going to ask her what her problem is. Like that would ever happen.*

"Go for it." Peter must have seen her irritated expression. Bending close to her ear, he whispered like a little devil on her shoulder, "If she gets nasty, you've got me as backup."

Amanda shook her head.

Peter shrugged. "Suit yourself."

Amanda knew she needed to be more assertive. Hell, her family kept telling her she needed to put more starch into her backbone, but she was uncomfortable with the idea of confronting anyone.

The very thought made her nauseous.

"I wouldn't want to cause more of a scene than I already have," she whispered.

When the elevator doors opened to the twelfth floor, Amanda tried to make her escape. Stepping off, she felt Peter's hand on her waist, detaining her. She scooted out of the way to avoid the other passengers.

"Peter, I'll talk to you later." With a curt nod, Mark strolled to his office. The receptionists stopped talking to greet him as he passed.

Amanda's eyes followed Mark until he disappeared through the office door.

"Oh no, not you too!"

Amanda jerked her attention back to Peter and felt her face burn with discomfort. "I have no idea what you're talking about."

"You've fallen for him," Peter said, shaking his head sadly. "You'll have to get in line with the rest of the women on this floor."

Some good that would do her. She placed her hands on her hips and stared at Peter. "No, I haven't. Remember, I'm the levelheaded one that everyone comes to for help. His types," she pointed in the direction of Mark's office, "are the gorgeous women who parade in here, dressed to the nines and full of confidence." Everything Amanda wanted to be.

"Have you looked in the mirror lately?" Peter asked, tapping her gently on the nose. "You're better looking and a lot smarter. All you need are some tips on makeup and more daring clothes and you'll knock them dead."

"And a personality change."

"No, you don't. If you ever decide to come out of your shell, I'll volunteer myself and your pregnant cousin to be your bodyguards. With my height and Stephanie's roundness, we'll make one heck of a barrier. "

"And protect me from what?"

"Sweetie, from the guys who'll come knocking on your door." With a wave, Peter walked away.

There was no chance in hell she could become the woman Peter had just described. It would be wonderful if it were true, but utterly impossible. She would need a miracle. Amanda was sure that would never happen.

Amanda walked to her office, passing the semicircular reception area where Cindy and Misty patrolled the comings and goings of everyone on their floor. They reminded her of twins, with their short skirts, tight tops and shoulder-length, streaked blonde hair. It always amazed Amanda how much effort they put into gathering office gossip. If they put half as much effort into their jobs as they did chitchatting, they'd get some work done.

Amanda gave them her customary morning nod and kept walking. She took a fortifying breath and braced herself for their usual barrage of insincere compliments.

"I just love that black outfit on you," Misty smiled, showing off her perfect teeth.

Amanda smiled back. Sure she did. It was more like, *where the hell did you get such a drab outfit?*

"And the way you twisted your hair up this morning is trés chic," Cindy piped in.

"Why, only yesterday Greg was saying how slim you looked," Misty said.

So now she was a fat cow? Amanda flushed. This was just great, even the office playboy had been talking about her.

She smoothed her skirt over her ample hips and hurried past. She wished these two idiots would stop talking.

"That's not what he said!" Amanda could hear the disbelief in Cindy's not-so-quiet whisper. "He said that she was on the chubby side of voluptuous. And if she wasn't such a prude he'd make a run for her himself."

As if! That slime-bucket wouldn't make it to first base. She entered her office, glad to leave behind their chattering for the calm atmosphere of her private space.

Her feet sank into plush carpet as she circled her desk. Settling into her soft, leather office chair, Amanda picked up the mail, intending to start on it immediately.

Looking through a connecting doorway, she saw directly into Mark's office. Their offices had the same color schemes, with taupe-colored walls, luxurious deep blue carpets and natural, bleached wood furniture. The only differences between the two rooms were Mark's credenza, where his files—and a hidden wet bar—were stored, and the coffee machine that sat on top. There were also two light-gold leather chairs in front of his desk and a sofa along one wall, above which hung a large, sky-view photograph of a previous construction project.

Mark was on the phone, jotting notes. The sun shone through the window behind him, illuminating the red highlights in his wavy brown hair. The ends curled at his collar. Amanda smiled. He needed a haircut. Conscious that she was staring, she abruptly looked away, not wanting Mark to find her gawking.

Some mornings he'd follow her progress into the office, while other times, he was so engrossed with his work he didn't know she was there. It was because he kept tabs on everything that went on in the company that he was so observant.

It wasn't anything personal, his watching her. For Mark it was strictly business. From the prickling sensation at the back of her neck, Amanda knew she had diverted her attention in the nick of time.

It was as though he had radar. It didn't matter how quietly she entered the room, Mark knew she was there. She could feel his piercing blue eyes locate and zero in on her. Yet, his eyes didn't register her presence as he continued to talk on the phone.

God, she hated when he did that. It was nerve racking when she caught Mark thinking with that far-off look and staring right through her. It always left her flustered, her palms sweating. She wanted to march up to his desk, wave her hand in front of his face and yell, "Hello? I'm here."

His chiseled good looks made her weak in the knees, but Amanda made sure not to show it. She wasn't going to place herself at the end of a very long line of women vying for his attention.

Mark gave a distracted nod of acknowledgement as he concluded his telephone call. Amanda placed her purse beneath her desk and clasped her shaking hands on her lap, giving him a smile her Aunt Lilly would have called "ladylike". She wasn't sure what her smile looked like, but it felt stiff.

When decorating the office, Amanda had placed the desks at an angle so they could look at each other through the connecting door. This setup was great for working, but terrible on her nerves.

"That was the Vice President, commending you on the great job you did on developing our last job site. He said if you keep this up, you'd end up as one of the directors."

Amanda straightened in her seat and beamed at Mark, pleased that her hard work was paying off. At twenty-six, she was the company's youngest-ever assistant to the CEO. The

"Mouse, ha! I'm not a mouse. There's only one rodent in this office, you self-centered, good-for-nothing rat!" She was just warming up.

Abruptly stopping on a step, Amanda placed her hands on her hips. "I should just turn around, march right back up there and confront that overgrown baboon, instead of scurrying away like the mouse he said I was." She stomped back up the stairs.

Reaching the exit door to her floor again, Amanda grabbed the handle and froze. Breathing heavily, she squeezed the handle until her knuckles turned white. "Come on, you can do it! Just open the damn door and tell him what you think." Her hand wouldn't budge.

With a defeated moan, Amanda rested her forehead against the door. Her anger drained from her body. She was left a quivering mass of nerves. "Oh hell, who am I kidding?"

Turning around with a dejected sigh, Amanda descended the stairs at a slower pace. Reaching the ground-floor exit door, she gave it a hard shove. It hit the wall with a satisfying bang. "I always run in the opposite direction. And I hate it."

Leaving the coolness of the air-conditioned building, Amanda stepped into the summer sun. The heat overwhelmed her. It was a typical August afternoon for Toronto. Hot and humid. Immediately, her clothes stuck to her body.

Amanda marched to her car. "Mouse. I'll show him who's a mouse." If that was true, then why was she walking in the opposite direction?

Opening the door to her blue Honda Civic, a blast of heat hit her as she got in to start the car. She quickly opened the windows and turned on the fan full blast, hoping to push some of the hot, sticky air out. Her air conditioner was still broken. Beads of sweat trickled down between her breasts.

Her nylon suit adhered to her body, making her more uncomfortable than she already was.

Squealing into reverse, Amanda sped out of the company's parking lot. She defiantly pulled the pins out of her hair, giving it a shake and letting the wind play with it. With the humidity, it curled into soft ringlets.

"I act and dress the way I do because it suits me just fine. If I wanted, I could wear something risqué just like the best of them. I bet I'd pop some eyes open when they took a gander at mousy Amanda and her cleavage. That would give them a nice wake-up call." Her words were filled with false bravado.

Amanda turned onto her street and slowed down. Large oak trees lined both sides, forming a natural canopy. The dense leaves sheltered the playing children, providing a partial shade where the sun's rays filtered through. Parents sat on curbs, taking turns watching the kids.

Driving along the avenue, Amanda passed beautiful old homes and exhaled a sigh of contentment. "God, I love this neighborhood."

Over the years, the homes had been renovated, garages had been added, rooms erected. The exteriors of some had been stuccoed. Walkways had been re-laid with flagstones, lending the area a more affluent look.

Front lawns held a profusion of plants and flowers in bloom. A gentle breeze carried the smell of roses and cooled off her heated skin. The serenity of her surroundings soothed her.

Close to home, Amanda gave a sigh of resignation. "Who am I kidding? I don't make waves and I wear the clothes I do so I can blend into the background."

She turned into her driveway and a two-story Victorian home came into view behind large weeping willow trees. It had a gingerbread scroll that accented a charming turret located at the front of the house. Amanda spotted her sister under the covered front porch, relaxing on the wooden swing.

This late in the day, the side and back covered porches were already hidden under a lazy shade. Yellow and orange groupings of California poppies welcomed her at the front of the house. Amanda pulled into the driveway on the side of the house and parked in the garage, before heading back toward Sarah.

She had one leg tucked under her, while the other pushed against the wooden planks. "Come and take a load off your feet," she said, the swing swaying in a lethargic motion.

Amanda couldn't get over how different they were. While she got all her coloring from her Irish mother, her older sister got hers from their Sicilian father. With straight, jet-black hair that hung down her back and brown, almond-shaped eyes, she reminded Amanda of a gypsy, especially when she wore long flowered skirts and off-the-shoulder blouses.

Sarah's tall, willowy body was the total opposite of hers. Although Amanda liked her own curves, she wouldn't have minded some of Sarah's height so she could distribute her weight more evenly.

They may have been different in appearance but they had a very close relationship. They could sense each other's emotions and finish each other's sentences. Aunt Lilly said that in one of their previous lives, they must have been twins.

Walking along the flowered walkway in front of the house, Amanda inhaled the fragrance of English lavender planted along the borders. Wearily climbing the last few steps, she plopped down beside Sarah. The remainder of her energy evaporated. "God, what a day."

Leaning her head back, Amanda closed her eyes and enjoyed the to and fro motion of the swing and the gentle squeak of the chains. She toed off her shoes and gave a tired sigh. The playful chirping of the birds in the surrounding trees embraced her.

After a few moments, she straightened, peeled off her hot jacket and draped it over the side of the swing. Unbuttoning her cuffs, she rolled her sleeves up before reclining in a more comfortable position.

"Here you go." Sarah passed Amanda a tall glass of iced tea. "You're home early for a change."

Amanda pressed the cool dampness of the glass against her temple. "I worked through my lunch hour."

"Smart idea. You look beat."

"You don't have to tell me." Amanda took a sip of her drink. The cold liquid soothed as it slid down her parched throat.

"You're not just tired are you?" Sarah asked. "Something else is bothering you."

Opening her eyes, Amanda gave her sister a tired smile. "You're good. What gave it away?"

"You're distracted. So tell your big sister what's bugging you."

"At the end of the day, I overheard Mark talking to Greg." Amanda frowned when she remembered how he had sat on her desk and insulted her.

"Greg Norman?" Sarah snickered. "Let me guess, he was his usual charming self."

"The one and only. Anyway, Mark was saying what a competent assistant I was and Greg agreed with him." Amanda pressed the icy glass to her forehead, then down the sides of her face. "He then went on to say that I wasn't much to look at, that I was quiet as a mouse and that basically I was invisible."

"That about covers it."

"Gee thanks." Anger and regret warred within her. The workday had started off terrible with the insincere compliments she had received, and ended with well-meaning insults she didn't need to hear.

"You hide your light under a bushel. Don't think I've forgotten that one night, when you were in college—you finally gathered your courage and wore one of my miniskirts and tops. You looked sensational and you had a bounce to your step. But when you returned home that night you were pale, your eyes were wounded. Since then I've never seen you wear anything but protective covering."

A far-off look entered Amanda's eyes. "Yeah, don't remind me." That evening had been traumatic for her.

She'd gone through hell trying to fit into her ex-boyfriend's narrow ideal. Each time she had tried to step over the lines, she was made to feel like a failure. Fearing rejection, Amanda had kept her body and personality hidden, suffocating the vibrant person within, afraid that she wouldn't be liked for who she was.

On the night Sarah referred to, Amanda had been paraded around the room, told to get drinks and made to feel worthless. While her ex had laughed with a group of people, she had grabbed her purse and left.

Sarah let out a heavy sigh. "You've got to stop hiding and learn to trust. Not every man is like that idiot you dated in college. The jerk tried to change you into something you weren't. I remember how you used to jump when he called. When you finally stood up for yourself, he nearly destroyed you. It took a lot of courage to walk away."

Amanda took another sip of her tea and listened to the ice cubes rattle in her glass as her sister continued to talk.

"After that night, it was like the other Amanda never existed. You just packed her away, along with your one colorful outfit. I would love to see you wear something like that to work," Sarah said.

Amanda pushed against the wooden porch and set the swing swaying. "People don't wear clothes that daring to work." From Sarah's skeptical look, Amanda knew she wasn't buying it.

"Girl, where have you been? Haven't you seen what the women at your office wear? Loosen up a little."

Amanda unbuttoned the top two buttons of her shirt. "Oh, I know you're right. But most of the skirts are too short and the tops are too tight and revealing." Amanda was certain that she would be uncomfortable wearing anything like that at work.

Besides, she preferred safe suits where no one could guess what she really looked like underneath. And no one ever paid attention to her.

Sarah gave Amanda an encouraging smile. "That's the whole point. They'd finally get to see what a knockout you really are. Just say the word and I'll take all those old clothes and hide them somewhere you'd never find them again."

Amanda was tempted, but she was terrified of taking such a drastic step as changing her appearance. People would notice. "I'm sorry, I can't wear attention-catching clothes like you. We're totally different. You're tall and slim while I'm short and chubby." Amanda swatted a fly away before it could land on her knee.

"Says who? You remind me of an auburn-haired Marilyn Monroe waiting to happen." Sarah chuckled. "I'd love to see their faces when you walked into the office."

Amanda's resolve weakened. She would love nothing better than to toss the old Amanda out and let a brighter, livelier Amanda step forward. "I like the way I dress." Boy could she lie. Thank God her sister couldn't see inside her head.

She dreaded what Sarah could do to her wardrobe. It wasn't that she had bad taste in clothes. It was that Amanda couldn't visualize herself in the clothes her sister wanted her to wear. Amanda really didn't have to think about it. She already knew the answer. No.

From inside the house, Amanda heard her aunt's heavy footsteps descending the stairs. The front door burst open and her aunt stepped onto the porch.

"Delicious, simply delicious," Aunt Lilly said. Her gray hair stuck up in every direction and the flowered dress covering her short, round proportions was caked in dust.

Aunt Lilly wore an angelic smile on her face that didn't bode well. It always meant that she was hatching one of her scatterbrained plans. Amanda couldn't figure out how a woman of Aunt Lilly's advanced age could get into so much trouble.

Aunt Lilly presented the girls with an old, dust-covered book. "Look what I found in the attic." She blew on the cover, sending puffs of dust into the air.

Amanda coughed and waved her hand in front of her face. "A family album?" She wasn't sure why her flustered aunt was so excited.

"Oh, no," she said, her eyes dancing with glee. "Something much better. It's a book of spells. Isn't that wonderful? It belonged to my dearly departed sister, Matilda." Aunt Lilly clasped the book to her chest. "Matilda traipsed around the world, while I was the homebody. She brought some interesting things back from her travels."

"I'm sure she picked it up at a tourist shop," Amanda said, holding out her hand for the book. "Why don't I return it to the attic?" She'd make sure to hide it in a safe place so her aunt wouldn't find it again. She could already see the wheels turning in her aunt's head.

"Oh, no." Aunt Lilly hugged the book tighter. "Tonight I'm going to cast a spell."

"Please don't be ridiculous," Amanda said. "Why would you want to do such a thing?"

"So that you can get your life in order, and to help you find the man of your dreams."

"Me? Why me?" Amanda's heart jumped. "What about Sarah? I'm quite content with the way my life is." It might be boring, but at least it was safe.

Aunt Lilly snorted. "Sarah doesn't need my help. You do. She attracts men like bees to honey."

Tell me about it. Amanda narrowed her eyes at the magic book and tried to figure out a way to get it out of her aunt's hands.

"I know you mean well, but do you really believe in that hocus-pocus stuff?" Sarah asked.

"I'm always open to new ideas. I'll get everything set up and both of you will help to see that nothing goes wrong." Aunt Lilly moved toward the door.

"Nothing?" Amanda asked skeptically. "Like the time you tried making that Italian rice dish and accidentally added a bottle of vanilla bubble bath, thinking it was extra virgin olive oil? The kitchen overflowed with bubbles."

Aunt Lilly frowned. "The bottles looked the same to me."

"Or the time you 'fixed' the vacuum cleaner and made it work in reverse? It looked like we had more dirt inside the house than we had snow outside that entire winter," Sarah said.

"So, what are a couple of slip-ups to a seventy-five-year-old woman? With both you girls there, what could possibly go wrong?"

Amanda still didn't like the idea. But nothing she said could convince her aunt otherwise.

"I'm off to round up all the things I'll need. While I do that, why don't you girls both take nice long showers? It always relaxes you after a hard day at work, and after dinner I'll cast my spell," Aunt Lilly said, dashing back into the house.

The bang of the door vibrated around Amanda, sending cold shivers along her heated skin. An uneasy feeling settled in the pit of her stomach. "I don't like this."

"Look on the bright side," Sarah said.

Amanda stood up and stretched. "Which is?"

"At least this time we'll be there to make sure nothing happens." Sarah picked up the tray of glasses and followed her to the door. "It'll be a piece of cake. Knowing Aunt Lilly, she'll light one or two candles, recite a poem and the dear will be happy."

Amanda opened the door and waved her through. "You make it sound too easy. We both know that there's nothing simple about Aunt Lilly."

"What's the worst that could happen?"

"If you have to ask, then we're in trouble."

Chapter Two

ഓ

After dinner, Amanda cleaned the kitchen while Aunt Lilly prepared for the spell she was determined to cast. She scrubbed until all the dishes were put away and the almond-lacquer cabinets gleamed. She paused to admire the crown moldings, pilasters and carved corbels before giving the granite countertops a final wipe.

Amanda let out a satisfied sigh. "Perfect." Everything was in order, just the way she liked it. Wiping her hands on her old shorts and baggy top, she grabbed a container of chocolate chip ice cream from the freezer and a spoon and headed for the parlor.

With each leisurely step, Amanda savored her ice cream, letting each spoonful melt in her mouth. Sarah was right, nothing would go wrong. Amanda stopped in the doorway and glanced around the front room.

She loved this room. Its old-fashioned ambience embraced her with its deep red walls and antiques. Red velvet sofas flanked an ornate marble-top table in front of the cast iron fireplace. The ceiling moldings were elaborately carved with vines and birds, glazed in the same light gold color as the ceiling.

It reminded her of a high-class gambling saloon or bordello with its crystal chandelier and cherry-colored upright piano against one wall. In front of two tall, lace-covered windows was a small round table, crowned with a Tiffany lamp and flanked by two gold, deep-buttoned medallion Queen Anne armchairs where men could have awaited their pleasures.

"Are you all set?" Amanda asked.

For this auspicious event, Aunt Lilly had set the table by the fireplace with a large assortment of colorful candles, flowers and a marble bowl.

Amanda turned to Sarah with raised eyebrows. "Two candles, you said."

Sarah gave an indifferent shrug.

Her aunt had changed into a man's red smoking jacket and had wrapped a white silk shawl around her head, turban-style. Both long-lost remnants from the attic, Amanda suspected. Sarah lounged in one of the chairs in front of the open windows, wearing her silk blue kimono and a towel wrapped around her damp hair.

Amanda sat in the remaining chair by the window, the container of ice cream on her lap. "Aunt Lilly, is that exactly what you'll need for your spell?"

Aunt Lilly continued setting up more candles around the marble dish. "No, not exactly."

"What do you mean 'not exactly'? Aren't you supposed to do things the way it says in the book?" Sarah asked.

"I think the book said to light a yellow candle for personal power, a red one for love and a green one—or was it blue?—for clarity."

Amanda gave her sister an anxious glance, as their aunt continued talking.

"The spell book was too complicated for me," Aunt Lilly said. "It wanted you to use different flowers for each spell and to light the candles on different days of the week and only if the moon was in a certain phase. I don't have time for that nonsense. So I made things simpler."

Amanda eyed the over-abundance of flowers and candles. "How?" This is what her aunt considered uncomplicated?

"I gathered all the different candles we had in the house and an assortment of flowers from the garden. I figured that if I lit all the candles at once and cast the spell, I'd cut the risks of anything going wrong in half," Aunt Lilly said.

Sarah raised her eyebrow. "Now there's a thought."

This was just great. Amanda's stomach knotted just thinking of the possibilities. She already had all the bad luck she could handle. She didn't need her wacky aunt adding to it. Amanda could see that Aunt Lilly was really getting into her role.

"With the moon being full, think of the success rate I'll have. And to top it all off I've written my own spell."

"Let me see it," Amanda said, rising from her chair, but her aunt waved her away.

"Later," she said, tapping the spell book in front of her. "I wrote it on one of the blank pages in here. You've have plenty of time to look it over."

"Do something," Amanda pleaded with Sarah. This was getting out of hand. Her stomach clenched tight as she watched her aunt fret over her display.

Sarah waved Amanda's concern away. "Take it easy. There's no such thing as magic. Since it's all nonsense, what difference does it make if she does it her way or not? She's harmless."

Amanda scooped a spoonful of ice cream into her mouth for courage. "You're no help," she said and turned back to her aunt. "Weren't there any spells in the book that you could have used?"

Aunt Lilly grunted away Amanda's suggestion. "Sure there were, but they had no kick to them. So I chose the sentences I liked and spiced them up a little."

"This is just great," Amanda said, spooning another mouthful.

Sarah yawned. "Amanda, you worry too much. She's going to light a couple of candles, recite her spell, blow them out and that's the end of it. Then we'll hit the sack."

Amanda lifted her spoon to take another mouthful, but dropped it back down. She was starting to feel sick. She wasn't sure if it was from nerves or from the amount of ice cream she had eaten. "Do I have to spell it out for you? We're talking about Aunt Lilly here."

Amanda jerked at the sound of Aunt Lilly's clap for attention. "Ladies, please, I need quiet to begin."

Amanda sat on the edge of her seat. "I wouldn't get too comfortable if I were you," she said with a glance toward Sarah.

It bothered her that Sarah wasn't taking this more seriously. How could she just sit there carelessly lounging while Amanda was so wound up? The apprehension that had settled in the pit of her stomach took residence there.

With cold fingers, Amanda placed the container on the small table. Taking a deep breath, she clasped her hands together and hoped that this would go quickly.

Aunt Lilly gleefully rubbed her hands together and lit the candles. She then placed a pair of Amanda's gold earrings in a bowl. "This is so exciting."

"Lucky you," Sarah smirked at Amanda.

Aunt Lilly raised her hands over the assembled candles and began her incantations.

"What you think is what you say,

For the spell to work this way."

A sudden puff of wind rushed through the open windows, making the drapes flap madly. It sounded like loud applause announcing the arrival of a presence. Swirling about, the current of air caressed the room and traced goose bumps up Amanda's arms.

What the hell? Amanda rubbed her arms as a shiver shook her body. It had been a clear night. Perhaps a storm was coming. Amanda debated whether she should get up and close the window, but didn't want to interrupt her aunt.

"Right or wrong, express your right,

All your thoughts brought to light."

The candles flickered, casting strange shadows on the walls. The storm must be getting closer. Wrapping her arms about her waist, Amanda wished her aunt would finish with the dramatics.

"Show the one that you desire,

How to light your inner fire."

The force of the wind increased, making the chandelier clink loudly as it swayed from side to side. Prisms of light danced around the room.

A rumble sounded in the fireplace as the gust of air escaped up the chimney. Was that thunder? Amanda hoped her aunt would finish before the storm hit. Otherwise, the carpets would get wet.

"Once everything is said and done,

Then you'll find your only one."

Candles rocked and toppled over, scattering the flowers. A doily caught fire.

"Oh my God!" Amanda exclaimed, grabbing the ice cream container and, with hands that trembled, pounding away at the flame with spoonfuls of ice cream. "I knew something like this would happen."

Sarah yanked the towel off her head and smothered the fire. "Nice one, Aunt Lilly," she said, collapsing back in her seat.

Amanda's heart hammered away in her ears. She waved at the smoke in front of her face and coughed. "Oh Lord, she's done it again!"

When the air cleared, Amanda stared at the toppled flowers and candles. Colorful splatters of wax mixed with large blobs of sticky ice cream, dripping from the table onto the floorboards.

Amanda tried to catch her breath as shockwaves of disbelief and something that felt like an electrical charge crept up her back, making the hair on her arms stand on end. "What was that?"

Sarah looked as dumbfounded as Amanda felt. Her aunt, on the other hand, was thrilled.

Aunt Lilly put her hands on her chest. "Oh my, wasn't that something."

Amanda slumped into the chair next to her sister. Her energy dissipated, leaving her limp and tired. Above, the chandelier continued to sway gently. Where the hell had that wind come from and where had it gone?

"It was something, all right," Sarah said.

Amanda was certain there had to be a logical explanation for what they had just witnessed. "The wind was a fluke, right?"

Sarah gave an uncertain shrug. "Beats me."

Amanda couldn't handle any more upsets. Her life was difficult enough without other forces interfering.

"That, my dears, is what you call the power of magic." Aunt Lilly sat down on the velvet sofa beside the fireplace and fanned her flushed face.

"That's it. I've heard enough," Amanda declared, pushing herself out of her seat. "What this is, is a bunch of hogwash. There's no such thing as magic. I'm tired and it's late." With quick agitated movements, she tidied up. "Let's clean this mess, so we don't have to look at it tomorrow morning."

The quicker she got rid of this disaster, the faster she could put it out of her mind. "I mean, magic? Really." She'd chalk it up to another of her aunt's escapades. "There's no such thing as magic."

"Sure. Anything you say." Sarah stared incredulously at the candles.

"Well?" Amanda planted her hands on her hips. "Are you going to give me a hand?"

"I'm coming," Sarah said, but didn't budge.

Amanda glowered at her aunt. "This is another of your catastrophes," she said, scraping the melted wax off the table with the tip of her nail.

"Hey, you don't have to be so abrupt with her." Sarah got up and gathered the flowers into her arms. "She was only trying to help."

Amanda pointed to her aunt and glared at her sister. "Now *you're* starting to sound as logical as she does." Amanda was not in a charitable mood. She lived with two women who both had screws loose.

Sarah snorted. "When have *you* ever been anything *but* logical?"

Amanda flushed with resentment. "Well, someone has to keep things running smoothly around this crazy house."

Aunt Lilly's gruff voice cut in. "Girls! Listen to you! You sound like a pair of hens fighting over the rooster."

Amanda gasped. What was wrong with her? She'd never snapped at her sister like that before. "Oh hell Sarah, I'm so sorry." She was overreacting. There was absolutely no reason why she was behaving so badly.

Sarah chuckled. "Don't mention it. Aunt Lilly, I can honestly say this was your best blunder yet."

high-rise condominiums. She tilted her head to the side and narrowed her eyes in concentration.

"What do you think?" Mark asked. He had loosened his tie and held a bottle of water in his hand.

Amanda looked around. "Were you talking to me?" She crossed her fingers behind her back. *Please don't let it be me.*

"Yes, you." Mark's smile widened. "I asked you what you thought of the drawings."

She should have escaped when she had the chance. "Something's not right."

"Excuse me?" Mark's smile disappeared.

"You asked me what I thought and I told you." Amanda inched backward toward the door. "Something is missing."

Mark gently stopped her and pulled her aside to whisper in her ear, "Now you tell me? Why couldn't you have said this before?"

"Because I wouldn't have mentioned it before," she said blushing furiously, everyone in the room staring at her.

"Now that you *have* brought it to our attention," Mark said with a tight smile, "maybe you can share your thoughts."

Share her thoughts? Like she had a choice?

The people in the room moved closer, awaiting her explanation. Amanda hesitated one final moment before moving to the front of the room. If only her mouth would act the way it was supposed to, she wouldn't be in this mess.

It was Mark's encouraging nod that gave her the go-ahead. The architect, a tall thin man with glasses and a goatee, came to stand beside her.

"When you look at the buildings, each one is beautiful and stands on its own."

The man smiled at her compliment.

"The two outer buildings are identical, with their semi-circular concave pattern near the top. In order to keep the center building as your focal point, I would reverse the pattern to form a gigantic wave, with the peak forming at the top of the middle and highest building."

Thank goodness she was wearing a long dress. Her knees were knocking together so badly, she didn't know how much longer they would hold her up.

The architect grew thoughtful. He held his elbow in one hand and stroked his beard 'til his eyes lit up with understanding. "She's right," the architect said, beaming at Amanda. "Would you like to join us for the remainder of our discussion?"

"No, I wouldn't like." She inched her way toward the door. "If it's all right with you, I'd prefer to head on out."

"But what if you have more to say on the matter?" asked the architect.

"Oh believe me, if I had anything else to say, you would have heard it already," she said and rushed out the door.

Chapter Three

ဆ

"AUNT LILLY!"

The bang of the front door sounded like a shotgun going off. The hall mirror rattled against the wall.

Frowning, Sarah walked out of her office and into the front hallway. "Is the house on fire?"

"I only wish."

Aunt Lilly came running from the kitchen, wiping her hands on her apron. "What's wrong?"

"What's wrong?" Amanda took a menacing step toward her aunt. "I'll tell you what's wrong. It's that damn spell! It's turning my life upside down."

Aunt Lilly placed her hands on her chest. "Oh my."

"Oh my, nothing." Amanda waved her finger in front of her aunt's face. "Get rid of it."

Aunt Lilly eyes widened. "I don't know how."

Amanda pulled at her hair. "It's simple. Light some more candles, recite a poem and get this damn thing off of me!" As Amanda's agitation rose, so did her voice.

"Take it easy," Sarah said.

"Take it easy? Have you any idea what kind of day I've had?" Amanda hit her forehead with the palm of her hand. "I should have turned the car around and driven back home this morning when I called the guy behind me a moron."

Sarah laughed. "You called someone a moron?"

Her aunt and sister were enjoying this. "This is not funny." Her nerves were shattered. Amanda slumped onto the bottom stair and hugged her knees to her chest. She couldn't possibly live like this. Day in and day out, not knowing what would come out of her mouth. "*Please*, Aunt Lilly, you've got to do something."

"Why don't you give the spell a chance?" Aunt Lilly smiled. "You might get used to it."

"I'm not getting used to anything." Amanda stood up from the step and marched her aunt backward toward the kitchen. "I want you to get your butt into the kitchen and start lighting candles."

Aunt Lilly's back bumped into the wall. "Party pooper." She gave Sarah a resigned expression. "And just when I was starting to like the new Amanda."

Amanda rushed through the kitchen to the back door. "Sarah, you get the candles while I get some flowers." She charged out the door and started pulling plants, roots and all, out of the ground.

"Hey, those are my yellow foxgloves and my red lupines!" Amanda could hear the anguish in her aunt's voice.

"I'll buy you more." Heat suffocated her body, drenching it in sweat. She pulled some lavender for good luck and ran back into the kitchen.

"How's this?" Sarah had filled the counter with candles.

"Are those all the candles in the house?"

"Every last one of them," Sarah said, leaning against the kitchen sink.

Amanda shoved the flowers into a vase, broken stems and all. "Okay." She rubbed her grimy hands on her dress. "Now it's Aunt Lilly's turn."

Her aunt twisted the front of her apron into knots. "I don't know what I should do or say to undo the spell."

"Try to do the opposite of whatever you did the first time, or say the words backward." Amanda encouraged her aunt with a smile she didn't feel.

"Fine, but don't go pulling any more of my flowers." Aunt Lilly lit a blue candle instead of a red one, a black one instead of a white one and tried to say the spell backward. "Yas ouy tahw si kniht ouy tahw…"

"Oh God," Amanda moaned, covering her face. It sounded ridiculous. She held her breath while her aunt spoke in gibberish then blew out the candles.

"How's that?" Aunt Lilly asked, pulling a chair away from the table and sitting down.

Amanda paused. "I don't know. I don't feel any different."

"It's not how you feel that counts but what you say," Sarah said, her eyes alight with mischief. "You're still going to talk to people you don't know and insult people you do."

Amanda's head was pounding. "So ask me some questions already." The throbbing settled around her eyes. She was getting a tension headache. "You can take that smirk off your face. This is my life we're talking about. Show some sisterly compassion," Amanda said, rubbing her temples.

"Sorry," Sarah said unconvincingly.

"Don't mention it." Sarah's mischievous smirk was starting to annoy her. Her sister was getting a kick out of this while Amanda felt absolutely miserable.

There was nothing to be happy about here. Amanda clasped her hands together to stop them from shaking and resigned herself to this crazy experiment. "Fire away," she said, taking a deep breath and waiting for her sister's question.

Sarah rubbed her hands together gleefully and asked, "Where did you keep your journal when we were growing up?"

Amanda paled—she couldn't stop herself from talking. "Beside the window there's a loose floorboard. If you lift it, you'll find it there." She was starting to feel sick.

"Damn, I always wondered where you put that thing," Sarah said.

Amanda's apprehension grew. She didn't like what was happening. She ran her hands up and down her arms to warm up. It frightened her to think that anyone could sneak into her head and find her most guarded secrets.

"Are you telling me the truth?" Sarah's grin turned sly.

Amanda sadly nodded. "Yes. Ask me another question. Maybe if I clamp my teeth real tight I can stop myself from talking."

Sarah snorted. "Yeah right."

From the look of her sister's face Amanda knew that she was about to spring a trap.

"When's the last time you had a sexual fantasy about your boss and how good was it?"

An overpowering tingle filled her mouth. It didn't matter how hard she clenched her teeth, the words poured out. "Last night. And on a scale of one to ten he was an eleven." Amanda clasped her hand over her mouth. "Oh, God help me!"

Aunt Lilly disguised her laugh behind a cough while Sarah held her sides, threw back her head and howled.

Closing her eyes, Amanda took short, quick breaths. She was falling apart. Her eyes may not have believed what had happened in the front room last Friday, but there was nothing wrong with her hearing. She heard everything that she was saying. The problem wasn't with her ears, it was with her mouth.

Sarah hooted. "OH MY GOD! This is *exactly* the kind of thing that'll happen at the office." Sarah pushed herself away from the counter and drew up beside Amanda. "Anytime someone asks you a question you'll be forced to answer it. Maybe I'll come with you to work this week to see what happens," Sarah said, patting her hand.

Amanda's nerves were frazzled. It didn't matter how hard she tried to stop the words from coming, they simply slipped out. "I'm doomed." Her eyes began to water.

Sarah sobered. "Sorry about that."

"I just don't get it." Amanda clasped and unclasped her hands. "How can a bunch of candles, some flowers and a poem control the actions of another human being? What am I supposed to do when I go to work?" Just the thought of what could happen frightened Amanda. She would be at the mercy of others.

"Avoid everyone," Aunt Lilly said.

"That's not possible with my job. I talk to a lot of people on a daily basis. I'm not walking around with this curse, or whatever you want to call it, stuck to me for who knows how long," Amanda declared, refusing to give up.

Sarah crossed her arms over her chest. "Tell me something? What are the chances of our dear aunt getting it right the first time and being able to take it off the second time around?"

"A million to one." Amanda dropped into the chair next to her aunt and clasped the woman's hands in a grip that transmitted her desperation. "That's why I want her to keep trying."

"Fine, but I can't concentrate with you looking over my shoulder like this." Aunt Lilly stood up and pulled Amanda to her feet. "Go and do something. Anything. Change out of your work clothes and just stay out of my way." Aunt Lilly pushed Amanda out of the kitchen.

Amanda became a whirlwind of activity. With frantic movements, she dusted and vacuumed the house, then went outside and watered the garden. Each time she returned to see how things were going, she received a negative shake of the head from her aunt and a not-so-apologetic shrug from her sister. Throwing her hands in the air, Amanda decided to paint the garage door. It was already dark outside, but she needed to keep her body and mind occupied.

An hour later, unable to stay away, Amanda peeked into the open window and saw her Aunt Lilly holding her hands over lit candles, while her sister looked on with skepticism. Leaning in closer she heard the words her aunt spoke.

"Under the full moon I did cast,

A spell for Amanda, whose words now spill too fast.

Please undo what I have done,

Even though my niece is now so much more fun.

Reverse the spell once and for all,

And bring her words to a silent lull.

Return her to her natural state,

Because my damn feet hurt and it's getting late."

Oh God, help me. Amanda looked up at the heavens before walking away. If that was the best her aunt could do, she was in big trouble.

The next time Amanda checked on their progress, her hands and arms were covered with splotches of dark brown paint. "Well? How are things going?"

"I could ask you the same thing," Sarah said. "You look like you've got chicken pox."

Amanda wiped her hands on her shorts. Chicken pox would be better than a spell, any day. "Keep trying."

"What do you think I've been doing?" Aunt Lilly asked. "Playing?"

"I can see you're not." Pots and pans were filled with peculiar-smelling liquids. Amanda didn't even want to know what her aunt had put in them. All sorts of flowers and colored candles with burnt wicks were scattered around the kitchen.

The situation looked hopeless. If her aunt failed, and Amanda didn't even want to think of that possibility, she would have to come up with a plan of her own.

"Maybe there's something you haven't thought of," Amanda said. But from the look of the kitchen she doubted it.

Aunt Lilly wiped her hands on her apron. "What else can I do? I don't know about you, but it's close to midnight and I'm pooped," she said, dropping into a chair.

Amanda refused to give up. The very thought of going to work the next day scared her. "That last spell I heard you working on, the one about lulling words and getting late, sounded promising to me. Do you think it worked?"

Aunt Lilly heaved a sigh of resignation. "Sarah, ask your sister something. I'm too tired to even think." She slumped further into her chair.

Sarah leaned against the counter. "If Mark asked you on a date would you go out with him?"

"Absolutely." Amanda clenched her fists. Damn, damn, damn. There it went again. Blasted words kept leaping out of her mouth.

Sarah snickered. "Oh yeah, she's still cursed."

"Does Mark know how you feel?" Aunt Lilly asked.

Amanda placed her hands on her hips and glared at her aunt. "No, he doesn't, and he isn't going to find out either!"

Sarah smiled. "Unless he asks you."

"He won't." Amanda's face grew hot with embarrassment.

"How do you know?" Aunt Lilly asked.

Amanda lost her patience. "I just do. If he hasn't shown any interest yet, what makes you think he's going to change? I'm the one afflicted by this spell, not him. If he catches me acting weird, he'll just think I'm nuts."

Defeated, Amanda collapsed into a chair, the remainder of her energy deserting her. She desperately needed a miracle here.

"Aunt Lilly, please concentrate and try again."

Amanda felt like a tightly wound clock spring. Her agitation continued to grow until it overwhelmed her. The very thought of what a nightmare tomorrow would be sent her into a breathless panic.

"I've tried everything I could think of dear." Aunt Lilly took off her bifocals and rubbed her eyes. "I've used all the types of flowers we have in the garden and I've lit every candle we could get our hands on."

"Let's face it kid," Sarah said, reaching into the fruit bowl, grabbing an apple and taking a large bite, "you're stuck with it."

"Stuck?" Aunt Lilly's eyes popped open. "That's it! I'll use glue." She stood up from the table. "You know, the kind that bonds really well? I'll set it on fire."

"No!" Amanda grabbed hold of her aunt's arm and sat her back down. "One fire a week is plenty. It'll blow up in your face."

"Just like this spell," Sarah said.

Amanda groaned. "Please don't remind me."

"Sarah, show some compassion." Aunt Lilly patted Amanda's arm. "Don't fret so, dear. Why, if I was thirty years younger and could speak my mind, I'd be in heaven."

Sarah chuckled. "You mean fifty years younger, don't you? And you already have an overactive mouth."

Aunt Lilly puffed up her chest. "Never you mind. Men today like older women who are outspoken and experienced."

"What experience do you have?" Amanda asked.

Aunt Lilly placed her hands on her hips. "I'll have you know that in my day I gave the men a run for their money."

Amanda gently patted her aunt's hand. "You mean you ran so fast that they couldn't catch up to you?"

"Oh, behave. All I'm saying is that instead of waiting for the man to do the chasing, you do it. If you reel in one of those slippery suckers, do what comes naturally. If you want to go out, ask him out. If you like something about him, tell him. And if you want to jump his bones, then hop to it."

Amanda slumped back in her seat as her mouth dropped open. "Well, I'll be." Who would have thought her sweet, innocent-looking aunt would think like that? Much less say the words "jump his bones".

"If you ask me, today's men have been given so many green lights that have turned out to be red, and vice versa, the poor dears don't know if they're coming or going," Aunt Lilly said.

Sarah chuckled. "You know, if you were fifty years younger, I'd feel sorry for the men in this city."

"At the same time, I could teach the two of you a trick or two," Aunt Lilly said.

"Right now I'm getting a kick out of this spell, because your last attempt at reversing it didn't work and Amanda looks like she's about to kill someone," Sarah said.

Aunt Lilly smiled sympathetically. "You could always look on the bright side."

"Which is?" Amanda was skeptical that her dear, absentminded aunt would come up with some logical advice.

"The next time anyone tries to step on you, you're going to put them in their place. Then they'll think twice before calling you a mouse," Aunt Lilly said.

Amanda's eyes widened. "You know about that too?"

"Of course I do."

"Can't anyone keep a secret in this house?"

"Not anymore," Sarah said, taking another bite of her apple.

"I was in the attic with the window open and eavesdropped on your conversation. I heard everything you and your sister said. You should hear the tidbits I pick up at the grocery store when no one thinks I'm listening," Aunt Lilly confided. "By the way, I never did like your ex-boyfriend. He reminded me of a strutting peacock, always preening himself. If his neck had been long enough, he would have kissed his own butt."

Amanda put her head down on the table. "Oh God, I'm ruined."

Aunt Lilly smoothed her hair. "I'm sure you're overexaggerating. Besides, the way you dress no one ever pays attention to you."

"Thanks," Amanda mumbled into her arms. She didn't know what to make of her aunt's insult-compliment. "I think I dress just fine."

"Please." Aunt Lilly sounded disgusted. "You try so hard at being invisible I'm surprised no one's plowed into you yet. Believe me, you have nothing to worry about."

Amanda lifted her head off the table. "You think so?" She needed all the reassurance she could get.

"Ah ha." A smile lit Sarah's face. "That's it. I'm going out and getting you something nice."

"Fine." Amanda knew when she was licked. "But nothing drastic."

Sarah's face lit up. "You mean it?"

Amanda could see from her sister's incredulous expression that she didn't believe her. She didn't believe it either.

Amanda gave a tired sigh. "Go ahead. When you're right, you're right. As a matter of fact, you can take all the clothes and shoes you think don't suit me and hide them. That way I'll have to wear the clothes that are left."

"I can't believe I'm hearing this."

Amanda shook her head to clear it. "You and me both." The spell must have impaired her reasoning. But if she really thought about it, what difference did it make what clothes she wore when she still managed to gain everyone's attention? "Just do me a favor and let me know when you do it."

"All right!" Sarah hugged Amanda.

Amanda returned her sister's embrace then dragged herself off the sofa. "I'm off to bed."

Sarah watched Amanda leave before turning to her aunt. "How would you like to go shopping for clothes tomorrow?"

Aunt Lilly gave her a thumbs-up. "Count me in."

"We have to leave early in case Amanda changes her mind. She could always stop us at the last minute. Then when she isn't looking I'll do the switch, so she's forced to wear what we get her. "

"Where should we say we went?" Aunt Lilly asked, shutting the kitchen light off and entering the hallway.

"I don't know. What do other people say when they're trying to cover their tracks?" Sarah asked as they made their way toward the stairs.

"Well, women usually say they're going shopping. But with us, it would be the truth. Men cover their tracks by saying they're going golfing, fishing or out with the guys. Which excuse would you like to use?"

"Golfing?" Sarah suggested. They'd go shopping, and the sooner the better. There was no way in hell she would warn Amanda, just in case she changed her mind.

Aunt Lilly pushed her glasses back up to the bridge of her nose. "Golfing it is."

The next morning, Amanda indolently stretched under her covers and felt the cool smoothness of cotton against her body. Slowly waking from a restless sleep, she listened to the sounds outside her window. When her senses returned, she remembered the previous night's events and moaned. Rolling over, Amanda tried to cover her head, but her tangled covers refused to budge.

With a huff, she checked the clock on her nightstand. Ten o'clock. No wonder the room was so bright. That's when she noticed a note propped up against her lamp.

Sitting up, she plumped her pillow against the headboard, pushed her hair back from her eyes and reached for the note.

Dear Amanda,

Saw that you were dead to the world this morning so we didn't want to wake you. Aunt Lilly and I have gone golfing. Enjoy your day.

Sarah.

Throwing the covers off, Amanda slid out of bed and stretched. "Golfing? Since when?"

After a quick shower, Amanda changed into a pair of denim shorts and a halter-top. In the mirror, she saw dark smudges beneath her eyes. "Coffee. I need coffee."

In the kitchen, a freshly brewed pot was waiting for her. Pouring herself a cup, Amanda stood by the sink overlooking the back garden and contemplated what she would do with her day. She decided to grab the spell book and head into the backyard to study it. Maybe she'd be able to find a way of reversing the spell.

Settling on a lounge chair, Amanda placed the book on her lap and flipped through it. Immediately, she noticed that each spell was precisely written.

"On a Tuesday, during a waxing moon, recite the following..." Amanda turned the page. "On a Monday, when there is a full moon, light a red candle..." Frustrated, Amanda slammed the book shut. "This is useless. How am I supposed to reverse a spell Aunt Lilly made up?"

Leaning her head back, Amanda closed her eyes and let the tranquil surroundings calm her nerves. After a restless night, the sun's soothing heat melted her tension and lulled her into a daydream.

Slipping into her fantasy world, Amanda wished Mark into her backyard. Like magic, he was there. This was great, at least in her daydreams she could be the boss. And best of all, she didn't have to worry about what she did or said.

Amanda's gaze leisurely traveled from Mark's bare feet to his wide-legged stance, over a pair of old gym shorts that were faded in some interesting areas, to finally rest on his arms crossed over his bare, muscular chest. Damn, he was magnificent.

Tilting his head, Mark squinted into the sun. "If we're not careful, we'll get burned." A bottle of suntan lotion appeared in his hands.

Without taking his eyes off her, he poured cream into his hand and rubbed it across his chest. He smoothed lotion over the defined lines of his muscles and kneaded the tops of his shoulders. By the time he finished, his upper body had a polished glow. Amanda raised her hands and fanned her heated face.

"Are you going to stand over there or are you going to join me?" Amanda held her breath as Mark slowly drew closer. She tingled with anticipation. When he finally stood beside her, she stared into a pair of eyes that gleamed with devilment.

Mark placed the bottle between her legs. Trailing a finger slowly up her inner thigh, he left a shiny trail of cream. Moving her legs to one side, he sat facing her. "Close your eyes and enjoy."

Shutting her eyes, Amanda's other senses magnified. "What are you doing?" Her ears strained to listen but she could only hear their breathing and the birds in the trees. The suntan lotion's fragrance teased her. She wet her lips and waited for whatever Mark planned next.

"No peeking," Mark said, slowly reaching out and gently tracing the shape of her lips with his fingertip. Gliding past her cheekbones, he massaged her temples and forehead in a circular motion. Finally, he reached the clip in her hair and carefully snapped it open. Amanda arched her neck, letting her hair tumble in curly disarray.

Mark threaded his fingers through her curls. "Such beautiful hair. It's a shame you always hide it." He let a soft curl twist greedily about his finger before letting go. He leaned forward and buried his face in her fragrant hair. Amanda sucked in her breath when his chest lightly brushed against her breasts.

He squeezed the back of her neck, slowly drawing his hands up toward the base of her skull and cupping them there. He repeated the motion until Amanda's head relaxed back and rested in the palms of his hands. Mark gently rotated her head from side to side. She felt boneless.

Amanda gave an appreciative moan as tension slowly seeped out of her body. She liquefied and sank deeper into the lounge chair. Absolute bliss.

Mark nipped her earlobe as he whispered, "It only gets better."

"Pour it on."

"The lotion or me?" Mark teased, removing the bottle between her legs. Amanda listened to the lotion being squeezed out of its bottle and gasped when he inserted it back between her legs.

"Both," she replied. Shifting in her seat, she felt a drop of lotion slip between her thighs. Reaching her limit, Amanda tried to take a quick peek.

"None of that," he said, lowering her fluttering eyelashes with his fingertip.

Small droplets fell on her arms and trickled down to the tops of her hands. Mark pried one of her hands off the chair and caressed lotion into her skin. Rotating his thumbs in small circles over the back of her hand, he applied firm pressure across her palm and wrist.

Entwining their fingers, Mark squeezed Amanda's fingers and slowly slid them through his own, pulling gently as he worked his way to the tips before letting go. Her hand dropped like a dead weight onto her lap. He then took her other hand and did the same.

Taking hold of the top of the bottle she still held between her thighs, Mark rocked it back and forth, letting her know where his hand was.

Amanda tightened her thighs as moisture pooled between them. Slowly prying the bottle loose, Mark spilled drops onto her legs, letting the beads of cream melt and slip down her legs to gather between her thighs. Amanda tightened her grip on the sides of the lounge chair. The less he moved the higher her arousal grew.

Amanda moaned. The heat from the sun raised her temperature and small drops of sweat formed on her brow. She was hot. So hot…

In the throes of her daydream, Amanda lifted her heavy arms and pulled her hair away from her neck. The breeze delicately dried her neck and formed goose bumps on her arms.

Amanda couldn't separate the heat of the sun from the heat that Mark created in her. She finally opened slumberous eyes and stared at Mark's flushed face.

He was as hot as she was.

With hands that shook, Mark untied her halter-top and let it fall to her waist. Pouring a generous amount of lotion into the palm of his hand, he rubbed it on the mounds of her breasts. Taking each hard nipple between his fingers, he rolled them back and forth, turning her body inside out.

Amanda arched into his caress as he teased his way down to her belly button. She sucked in a surprised breath when he applied pressure on her exposed flat stomach, making it quiver. Amanda's need rose a notch higher.

Vibrant blue eyes returned her stare. "Give me your hands." He cupped her palms and drizzled lotion into them.

"Whatever I do to you, you do to me," he said, placing her hands on his chest. Holding her wrists, he showed her exactly what he wanted. Back and forth, a slow rhythm began. Mark let go of Amanda's wrists and poured more lotion into his palms…

Writhing in the lounge chair, oblivious to her surroundings, Amanda's daydream heated considerably as she held her arms in the air, her hands rubbing lotion onto a body only she could see.

Each movement Mark made, Amanda mirrored. When he smoothed his thumbs along her collarbone, Amanda caressed hot skin. As his hands teased the tops of her breasts, Amanda willingly copied his movement.

When Mark leaned forward to lick her earlobe, Amanda edged closer. Anticipating his next move, Amanda sat forward…

...and nearly toppled off the lounge chair when the sound of a car horn blasted. Startled, Amanda found herself uncomfortably aroused and alone, her hands poised in the air.

Sitting up, disoriented, Amanda glanced around to see what had brought her out of her sensual imaginings. She heard a second car door slam. "That's great! The best sex I've had and I don't even get the guy in my own dreams," she growled, squirming in her seat.

Amanda leaned her head back and blew out a frustrated breath. Looking toward the sounds coming from the driveway, she caught a glimpse of her aunt waving frantically at her sister and wondered what those two were up to. She pushed herself off the chair.

Before she could take a couple of steps, her aunt rushed toward her holding her chest. "Where's Sarah?" Amanda asked, glancing toward the driveway.

"Oh, she just went in by the front door," Aunt Lilly replied, steering her back toward the lounge chair. "Were you practicing Tai Chi when we arrived?"

"No. What gave you that idea?"

"When we first drove up to the house we weren't sure if you were waving at us or doing those exercises I see seniors practicing in the park every Saturday morning," Aunt Lilly said.

Amanda felt herself turn a bright shade of red. "Oh...um, yeah, Tai Chi." Her dream lover had seemed so real.

Aunt Lilly patted Amanda's arm. "I think you'd better keep practicing because it didn't look like you were doing it right. It's supposed to relax you, not make you jumpy."

Amanda quickly changed the subject. "Did you enjoy your golf game?"

Aunt Lilly looked away. "Oh yes, we played a short game and decided it was too hot."

"So you played nine holes?" Amanda pressed, observing her aunt's guilty flush.

Aunt Lilly fidgeted with the pleats of her dress. "Yes, yes that's what we did."

Amanda grew suspicious. "So did you use your putter or one of your irons?"

"Putter? Of course we didn't dilly-dally. We went out and did what we had to do. And you know we keep our iron in the laundry room."

"What are you up to now?" Amanda was not going to get a straight answer.

"Nothing, absolutely nothing," Aunt Lilly replied as she looked everywhere but at Amanda.

She'd eventually find out whatever her aunt was hiding. She always did. Shrugging, she decided to head in. "I think I've had enough sun. Let's go inside for some lemonade."

"No!" Aunt Lilly blocked Amanda with her body. "You can't do that."

"Why not?" Amanda tried to sidestep her aunt, only to have her way blocked by a very determined, very wide woman.

"Because…" Aunt Lilly stalled, frantically searching the backyard. Her eyes lit up as they fell on the spell book.

"Because I want us to look over the book just in case we missed something," Aunt Lilly finished, steering her back to the lounge.

"Good idea."

Aunt Lilly tugged on her collar and longingly stared at the house. "I just hope it's not for long," she said, fanning her face.

"You hope what's not for long?" Sometimes her aunt didn't make sense.

"Why, your spell, dear. I hope it doesn't last too long."

"My sentiments exactly."

Chapter Four

ဆ

Mark dropped a T-bone steak into his shopping cart and sighed. He'd be making his own dinner tonight. The evening had started off with so much promise and had quickly deteriorated. He'd only wanted a quiet evening with Ashley to take his mind off work, while his current girlfriend had wanted to have a serious talk.

He should have seen it coming. He had entered her apartment and immediately the hair on his arms had stood on end. It wasn't so much the candles that had lit the room or the table set for two. It was the way Ashley kept sneaking peeks at him when she thought he wasn't looking that should have clued him into what would come next.

He cringed inwardly. It wasn't his fault that her feelings had changed while his hadn't. Still, he should have recognized the signs. It didn't change the fact that he felt like a heel.

At the beginning of each relationship he set the rules. Nothing serious. Some had enjoyed the arrangement, and still dropped by for a night on the town. It suited both parties. They conveniently scratched each other's itch.

Some women, however, believed they could change him. It ended in disappointment for the women and resignation for him. He couldn't change how he felt.

Not after the job his ex-fiancé had done on him. He'd worked side by side with Lauren, climbing the corporate ladder. Always helping her reach higher, push harder, feeding the avaricious gleam that he hadn't noticed in her eyes.

Looking back, Mark realized that she had gotten a high each time they closed a deal or made a hostile takeover. He felt sick watching her elation as he broke one man's dreams to pieces while fattening another man's pockets. It had reached a point where he didn't recognize — or like — the person he saw in the mirror.

When he had finally lost a deal, and didn't particularly care, their roads had separated. He hadn't even seen it coming.

At first she had made excuses about working late, and the sucker that he was, he'd believed her. 'Til the day she had breezed into his office, handed back her engagement ring and walked out of his life on another man's arm.

Another poor sucker destined to carry her further up the corporate ladder. Mark realized that he had served his purpose and she was now on to bigger fish.

He'd busted his butt getting their last successful deal and she had taken all the credit. She'd used him as a springboard. Last time he'd heard about her through the grapevine, she'd been appointed a director of the company she currently worked for.

Nowadays, Mark stayed away from business-pleasure relationships and kept all friendships on a no-strings-attached basis. He'd gotten into the habit of dating eye candy instead of intelligent women. Women who couldn't relate to him.

Mark figured that he couldn't pin himself down to someone with half a brain, yet couldn't commit to someone intelligent.

For the past two weeks he had been totally distracted by Amanda's behavior, completely missing Ashley's silences. He'd spent his days with an assistant who wouldn't shut up and said exactly what she thought, and his nights with a girlfriend who said too little, pretending their arrangement was fine but feeling the opposite.

Mark made his way down the dairy aisle and indiscriminately dropped a container of margarine into his cart. He spotted a middle-aged woman hurrying her overweight husband along, as the man kept his eyes glued to the woman standing in front of him.

He couldn't blame the guy. He had a back view of one hell of an amazing woman. She was oblivious to her surroundings as she listened to a headset and tapped her red sneakers to a steady beat. Her hips swayed gently from side to side, keeping time with the rhythm he could slightly hear thumping in the air.

Mark chuckled. The man must have heard, for he turned around and mouthed the word "wow" without letting his wife see, before disappearing around the aisle. Mark agreed with him—she was one hell of a package.

She wore red shorts and a white T-shirt that hugged her curved waist and flared over a set of voluptuous hips. The best was her hair. Soft red and gold curls reached the middle of her back. Amazing. Her whole body seemed to be alive. He watched the curtain of soft, full, flaming color swing back and forth.

Mark drew nearer. A fragrance teased his senses and he frowned. Where the hell had he smelled that perfume before? Mark inhaled again and searched his memory. A picture teased the outer edges of his mind, only to slip away. No big deal. It would come to him eventually.

In the meantime, there were more important things to think about. Like whether the woman's front was as delicious as her back.

Mark inched closer and purposely reached for the same yogurt container she did. Their fingers brushed and he felt her start.

Excited and eager, he summoned his most charming smile and deepened his voice, "I'm sorry, were you reaching for —" Mark began.

Then froze.

"Amanda?" His smile disappeared as the blood drained from his face before it came rushing back.

Absolutely not. No way. It couldn't possibly be her.

Amanda took her headset off. "Hi, Mark. Fancy meeting you here," she said through a strained smile. Amanda stood in front of her cart and moved from side to side, as if she was trying to block his view.

From nerveless fingers, the yogurt fell out of his hand and crashed to the floor. The lid exploded on impact, spraying Amanda across the front of her legs. She gasped as the cold pink cream made contact.

"Oh God, I'm so sorry."

"It's okay, really."

"Here, let me help you." Mark crouched to wipe her leg and hit his forehead against Amanda's as she bent over at the same moment.

"Ouch." Amanda straightened and rubbed her head.

"Ah, hell." Mark watched the yogurt slowly drip down her legs. "Let me clean that up for you."

"Really, I can do this," she said, moving aside.

"It was my fault." With the side of his finger he scooped a dollop of cream from her shin and caressed warm skin. Oh hell, this was terrible. She felt as good as she looked. Smooth, soft and sticky. Why couldn't she have forgotten to shave her legs or something? And why was he torturing himself, trying to clean all the yogurt he could find?

"Cut that out," Amanda exclaimed, slapping his hand away, making the yogurt he held splatter across the floor and over his shoes.

Mark straightened and held his hand away from his body, not sure how to clean it. "What are you doing here?" Jeez, was he smooth.

"Shopping." With her fingers, Amanda scooped the yogurt off her legs.

"Where are you going to put that?"

"In my mouth," she said and licked her fingers.

Mark couldn't believe the twirling action her tongue was doing. She reminded him of a tabby cat cleaning itself. Mark rubbed his hand on the side of his jeans.

When she bent to swipe more yogurt, her hair brushed up against his legs and sent his pulse racing. As if that wasn't enough, her shorts tightened around that lush butt of hers every time she leaned forward.

"I'm sorry about the yogurt. Is there anything I can do to help?" Like he hadn't done enough already.

"No!" Amanda straightened and walked around her cart. "I've taken care of it."

Damn, she was skittish. But what the hell was she doing now? She was pulling at the edges of her shorts, trying to lengthen them. When that didn't work, Amanda tugged at her T-shirt. It only emphasized her breasts. Mark wished she would stop her fidgeting. He did not want to notice these things about his assistant.

Lost for words and feeling like a fool, Mark just stared. This colorful, vibrant woman was his assistant? Sure he'd gotten teasing glimpses of what Amanda hid beneath those damn awful clothes of hers. But he still couldn't associate the woman who tortured her hair into a bun with the woman standing in front of him. He rubbed his face. "God, what a figure."

"What did you just say?"

Mark dropped his hands and stiffened. He hadn't realized he had spoken his thoughts aloud. "I said, go figure." His stiff lips formed what he hoped was a smile. "I meant, what are the chances I'd find you here shopping. It's a small world, isn't it?"

"I guess."

The walls were closing in on him. He needed to escape. "Well, don't let me interrupt what you're doing. I can see from all the ice cream in your cart, you must be getting ready to celebrate."

Amanda gasped and blushed furiously. Shit, he'd forgotten the comments she had made about being screwed and getting lucky with the checkout boy. He didn't want to make her more embarrassed than she already looked.

He needed to get the hell out of there. "Later." He took two steps back, pivoted around and tried not to run. He made it to the end of the aisle before he realized that Amanda was calling him.

"Mark?"

God, now what? He wanted to get as far away from her as soon as possible, so he could forget what she looked like. What she felt like. "Yes?" he asked, his grin hurting his face.

"You forgot your cart."

"You dumb cluck," Mark grumbled.

Amanda's eyes widened. "I beg your pardon?"

"Not you. Me." He retraced his steps as his face grew hot with humiliation. He tried to laugh it off but it sounded like a harsh bark. He steered the shopping cart around and pushed it forward. "See you at work on Monday in your usual clothes— I mean, like usual." He didn't wait for her response as he rushed around the corner.

Come Monday, Amanda would be back in her ugly clothes and he'd be able to forget about the whole incident. Thank God for small mercies. He wanted her to remain unnoticeable, designated to the insignificant corners of his mind, where she could be forgotten. He breathed a sigh of relief. Everything would return to normal. No more candid Amanda, no more soft curves.

Mark tossed the items of his cart onto the checkout counter and hoped the cashier would hurry.

Amanda had become a distraction that was ruining his orderly, logical way of thinking. First at work and now this, exposing curves that had no business being revealed. Her body could be registered as a lethal weapon with the police. She was his plain assistant and that's what she had to remain. What else could she possibly do to destroy his equilibrium?

"I don't need this."

"Sir? You don't want your change?" The cashier had his receipt and change in her hand.

"Sorry, I was talking to myself." Mark stuffed the money in his back pocket, grabbed his grocery bags and hightailed out of there.

He was in trouble. He was in terrible trouble.

By the time she went to bed Sunday night, Amanda was an absolute nervous wreck. All night long she'd stared at the ceiling, afraid to fall asleep. In her head, she'd gone over Mark's horrified reaction when he had bumped into her at the grocery store. "Oh, God!" she moaned, covering her head with her pillow.

Mortified by how desperately he seemed to want to escape, she had stood there, in her own hell, trying to hide her body and praying that he wouldn't notice the number of ice cream cartons in her cart.

He'd stared at her like a bug under a microscope. Had she really looked that bad? It must have been an unpleasant shock seeing her in her grubbies, her disheveled hair curling down her back.

Exhausted, she finally drifted off to sleep in the early morning hours—only to wake up late.

She had forgotten to set her alarm, and now would have to hurry to get to work.

She looked at her reflection in the washroom mirror and reapplied her eyeliner. She'd found the eyeliner in a brand-new makeup case with a tag attached that said, *For your birthday, love Sarah and Aunt Lilly.*

Amanda tightened the towel around her body and headed for her bedroom. Right now, her bedroom was the only calm in her chaotic life. It reminded her of an English rose garden with its cream-colored furniture and the soft pastel walls that matched the yellow rose-patterned bedcover. It was tranquil—something her life wasn't.

Amanda opened her closet and froze.

"Impossible!" She rifled through the colorful outfits. It didn't matter which way she pushed the hangers, her dull baggy outfits weren't there.

"Oh God." Cold tremors of shock shivered through Amanda's body. "This can't be happening to me." She dropped to her knees and opened one shoebox after another—black high-heeled sandals, stilettos, open-toe gold evening shoes, fuzzy pink slippers—not one sensible pair among the lot.

"AUNT LILLY!" Amanda yelled, racing to the stairs.

A chair scraped the floor, followed by the sound of slippers flapping. "Amanda dear, what's wrong?" Aunt Lilly called from the bottom of the stairs.

"My clothes," she gasped, one hand holding onto the banister for support, while the other clutched the towel against her pounding heart. "Where are my clothes?"

Aunt Lilly plastered an innocent smile on her face. "Oh, you found our surprise. Isn't it wonderful?"

"This is not what I'd call wonderful." She was so dizzy her ears were ringing. "Why didn't you say something?" Her knuckles turned white from the strength of her grip. "You were supposed to warn me before you did this."

"And ruin your surprise?" Aunt Lilly snorted. "Aren't the new outfits beautiful?"

"Yes, they are." *Shut up, Amanda, and think of something.* Amanda raised a shaking hand and rubbed her forehead. "Oh my God, oh my God, oh my God." The ringing in her ears worsened. This could not be happening to her. She had enough to cope with.

"When did this happen?"

"Last night, while you slept," Aunt Lilly chuckled. "You were always a heavy sleeper. Waking you up when you were young was like rousing the dead. This time your sleep habits came in handy. You didn't even stir when we turned on the lights to see what the hell we were doing."

"You—Sarah—" For the first time in weeks, Amanda was speechless.

"You're so happy that you're lost for words. You just go and put on one of your new outfits and come down so I can see how you look." Aunt Lilly was about to leave when she turned back to her. "Oh, I almost forgot."

From her gleeful expression, Amanda knew she was in for another unpleasant surprise. "Now what?"

"We also got you new undergarments."

"What? Sarah stole my bras and panties?"

"Not to worry, they're quite nice. Although I wouldn't call those small triangles underwear," Aunt Lilly said, shrugging. "But your sister said that everyone wears them." With a happy wave, Aunt Lilly padded back to the kitchen.

Amanda swayed at the top of the stairs. "My underwear? Sarah stole my underwear?" Amanda rushed back to her room. Yanking a drawer open, she stared at the assortment of colorful lingerie.

Beautiful underwire lace bras and matching thongs in taupe, black, red and purple filled her drawer. She caressed the lace and silk with a shaking finger. "Where are my sensible cotton granny panties?" She couldn't wear something as beautiful and sexy as this.

"When I get my hands on my sister I'm going to kill her. First I'm going to lock my aunt in a room where she can't cause any more damage, then I'll kill my sister," Amanda ranted.

Amanda gingerly lifted a red bra and looked it over. So where was the rest of it?

"I can't wear this," she decided, dropping the bra back into the drawer. "I'll call in sick and buy some more clothes." She pulled her fingers through her hair. "Oh hell, there are important reports that need to go out today."

She paced to the bed, then back to the lingerie drawer. "Damn, damn, damn. I'm talking to a bunch of underwear. Maybe I should just lock *myself* up."

Not having any other choice, Amanda grabbed the shocking red set again. Taking a deep breath, she threw off her towel and cautiously shimmied into them. It wasn't as though they would bite her, for Pete's sake.

Amanda could hear her aunt calling, "Hurry up, or you're going to be late. If you need me I'll be out back gardening." Soft footsteps walked away, followed by the back door closing.

Amanda took a deep breath and braced herself before looking at her refection. A hot flush infused her body. Pressing cold hands against her flushed cheeks, Amanda inspected herself from the top of her full breasts to her very exposed round bottom. She'd never seen her body in this type of packaging before.

"Oh my." Amanda's astonishment turned to happy disbelief. She proudly straightened her back, posing from side to side to admire her body.

Amanda cupped her breasts over the bra. "How am I going to hide these?" Twisting around, she admired the back view. Her blush deepened. "Not too shabby. I look like one of Mark's women." Amanda stilled as her words sank in.

A triumphant gleam entered her eyes as she scrutinized her image more carefully. With her shoulders back, Amanda felt empowered. No one would ever know what she was wearing under her clothes. She could walk around all day feeling naughty.

She raised her chin a notch. "I can do this."

Amanda rushed to her closet and pulled out the first suit that came to hand, throwing it on the bed. Pulling open her nightstand drawer, she found silk stockings in a nude color, instead of her regular gray and black pantyhose.

"Damn, Sarah took this room apart."

Sitting on the edge of her bed, Amanda slowly slipped on a stocking, enjoying the wicked sensation of silk against her leg before quickly slipping on the other.

Standing up, Amanda looked in the mirror and saw a stranger with sparkling green eyes staring back. Even her skin glowed. She pointed her toes and noticed that her legs looked much longer. She looked deadly.

"Next." She slipped on the little black number she had thrown on her bed. The skirt fell straight to just above her knees and hugged her hips. "Oh, hell." This outfit was the total opposite of what she usually wore to work. "Like I have a choice."

Next was a little jacket that buttoned in front. It hugged her waist and drew attention to the deep V at her cleavage. Looking down, Amanda realized there was too much of her on display. "Shit." All day, she'd wonder who was looking down her top.

Amanda pulled the edges of her lapels together to hide her breasts, but they only rounded further and seemed to pop out of the opening. "No way am I spending the day like this."

Amanda opened the drawer where she kept her scarves and hair clips. She found two notes from her sister. Where her scarves should have been, the first note read, *Don't hide your light under a bushel.* The second note said, *Warning, due to safety reasons, mainly mine, all pins and clips have been removed.* Her sister had signed it.

Amanda clenched her fists. "I'm not licked yet." She remembered seeing a lacy camisole hanging in her closet. Pulling it off the hanger, she threw off her jacket and slipped the camisole over her head. After she re-buttoned the jacket, she gave her reflection a final look. "Much better."

Thrusting her feet into a pair of high-heeled black pumps, she dashed out of her room and out the front door. She was out of time and options.

Head held high, she ate up the distance between the house and her car in quick, wide strides.

"You go, girl!"

Amanda spun around and spotted her aunt with an enormous smile on her face. "Who taught you to talk like that?" she asked.

"Oprah."

Amanda shook her head and jumped into her car.

All the way to work, Amanda kept her fingers crossed. "Please don't ask me anything, please don't ask me anything."

At this point, she was worried more for the people who dared cross her path. She had held so many things back, she pitied whoever got in her way.

Amanda parked her car and took a deep breath to calm her nerves. "I can do this." It was now or never. With her heart pounding and her body quaking, Amanda got out and locked her car. She prayed that she would make it to her office without a hitch.

She dashed into the building and stepped into the waiting elevator. Amanda caught some of the passengers staring at her via the mirrored doors. From their expressions, they loved her new image. Amanda released a breath slowly and relaxed. Maybe this wasn't going to be so bad.

With a secretive grin, Amanda admired her reflection and caught Agnes' disgruntled stare as she mumbled under her breath and pointedly stared at her cleavage.

One minute Amanda was facing the front of the elevator and the next, it felt like an invisible force spun her around, so that she faced Agnes. The next second her mouth started flapping. "Is there something I can help you with?"

Amanda slapped her hand over her mouth and groaned while the woman's eyes reflected the same intense humiliation Amanda had often endured. She dropped her hand away from her mouth, letting it continue on its natural course. "So sorry, I didn't quite catch what you said."

Agnes shook her head. "Nothing. It was nothing." She stepped back to stand against the elevator wall, closer to the other passengers.

With a stiff nod, Amanda turned around again and waited for her floor. Filled with nervous tension, she fisted her hands and prayed that she could get off the elevator without any more mishaps.

She hoped Agnes wouldn't open her mouth again. But as the elevator doors opened to her floor, she heard the spiteful words.

"Do you think they're real? She's never had them before."

Amanda whirled around and stopped the elevator doors from closing. "What was that you just said?" she asked, leaning toward Agnes in a menacing manner.

Taken by surprise, Agnes stammered, "I-I-I...said they were fake." She glanced at Amanda's cleavage in embarrassment.

"Lady, there's nothing phony about my body and if I had the time I'd show you. But then these lovely gentlemen would never make it to work on time." Amanda let the doors close on the poor woman's shocked face and the businessmen's chuckles.

Amanda rested her forehead against the wall. "I can't believe I just said that."

If she could make it to her office everything would be okay. Sighing, she pushed away from the wall and turned toward the reception area, stumbling to a stop. Greg and the receptionists were frowning like they didn't recognize her.

Taking a deep breath, Amanda plowed forward.

"Madame? Can I help you?" Misty asked, her voice sounding very respectful. Regrettably, Amanda stopped in her tracks. Damn, she'd almost reached her goal. "No thanks, Misty, I'm just going to my office."

"Do I know you?" Confused, the receptionist's eyes traveled over her tailored appearance.

"Of course you do." Amanda enjoyed their baffled expressions. Did she really look that different?

All three took a closer look. "Amanda?" they exclaimed as one voice.

"One and only." Now if she could inch her way out of their attention.

Three pairs of eyes watched her progress with varying expressions. Greg Norman wore a wolf-like sneer. Cindy's eyes were round and her mouth opened and closed like a fish trying to breathe. And Misty's eyes were maliciously narrowed as they gave Amanda the once-over.

Oh Lord, not again. At this rate she'd make her office by lunchtime.

"Well, well, well. I didn't know you had it in you. Or that there was so much of you to admire," Greg said, staring at Amanda's cleavage.

"And I didn't know *you* had a thing for mice, either." Amanda's comment wiped the insidious grin off Greg's face.

Misty pasted on a fake smile. "Amanda, I just love your outfit. Where did you get it?"

"Yes, I'd like to know too," jumped in Cindy.

Amanda's intention had been to pass them with a nod, but now she felt trapped. Her feet wouldn't budge, but her mouth didn't seem to have the same problem. "Thanks for the sincere compliments, ladies. I'll have to ask my sister where she bought it and I'll get back to you."

"Now, aren't you generous?" Greg hadn't unglued his eyes from Amanda's chest.

"Hey, buddy," Amanda said, clicking her fingers in front of his face, "kindly put your eyes back into their sockets." As far as she was concerned, this conversation was over. With a final nod, she turned on her heels and found her way blocked by Greg.

Amanda narrowed her eyes. "Do you mind?"

Greg smiled. "What's the rush? It's not like Mark will fire you."

"I'm late." At least that was the truth.

"Don't worry," said Greg as he advanced. "Besides, being coworkers, we should get better acquainted."

"That's so sweet of you." Her sarcasm was lost on him as he puffed up with conceit. "Thanks Greg, maybe some other time." She sidestepped him and headed to her office.

"How about lunch? I'm sure I can squeeze you in. So what do you say?"

Say? Oh, he shouldn't have said that. It would be a pleasure to let him know. Holding onto her office door, she quietly dropped her bomb. "When would you find the time? You're already dating both Cindy and Misty behind their backs. Were you intending to squeeze me in between the two of them?"

Greg flushed brightly.

The receptionists shrieked.

Misty confronted Cindy. "You're *what*?"

"How could you do this to me? I thought you were my friend," Cindy whined.

"Me? What about you? Sneaking behind my back with my boyfriend," Misty said.

"*Your* boyfriend?" Cindy yelled back. "He said he was *my* boyfriend."

Amanda slammed her office door and listened to the sounds of their angry footsteps as they screamed and called Greg names. There was a loud shattering sound as an object crashed against a wall, followed by the sound of running feet as the women chased Greg in the direction of the nearest exit.

Amanda cringed, but kept her ear stuck to the door. It sounded like a stapler had hit a wall.

An explosion of laughter erupted behind her. Spinning around, Amanda found Mark standing in her office.

"You know, I always wondered when Greg would get his just desserts. But I never figured it would come from you."

His grin disappeared as he cleared his throat. "Not that I blame the guy."

He looked like he had just gotten kicked in the stomach.

She stood still and endured Mark's scrutiny. His eyes slowly caressed her face, over her rumpled hair, slowly taking inventory of her transformation before finally settling on her eyes again. The silence between them lengthened, making her uncomfortable. He was pale one minute and flushed the next.

His confusion settled into a frown. For a guy that had just given a compliment, he didn't look too pleased.

"Greg's always been like that. But I don't have to put up with it," Amanda said, wishing he would blink.

"You don't like the guy very much, do you?"

Was he having trouble talking? Amanda watched his Adam's apple move up and down. "No, I don't."

"Any reason?"

Amanda moved away from the door and walked toward Mark. Her mouth tingled as the words poured out. "Besides being a louse, a cheat, self-centered and an octopus—no." Amanda watched Mark's expression darken.

"Wait a minute, 'octopus' as in hands?"

"Nothing serious." She couldn't keep anything to herself. "Just a pat on the behind. Don't worry, I know how to look after myself."

Mark raised his eyebrows in disbelief. "Since when?"

"Since two Fridays ago." Amanda crossed her fingers behind her back, hoping that he didn't ask any more questions. But that was wishful thinking.

"So you're not going to be a timid little m—" Embarrassed, Mark snapped his mouth shut.

Amanda narrowed her eyes. Heat rushed up her neck to fill her face. How she hated that label. "Mouse?" A thin chill hung to her word. "Go ahead, say it. But no more. You have a problem with that?" Amanda stepped forward and pushed Mark out of her way.

"No, not at all." His body jumped beneath her touch.

"Don't speak too soon, you might regret it."

Mark grimaced. "This transformation is…different. But I thought you liked your other clothes. What brought on these changes?"

"I hated my old clothes." Why did Mark look so miserable? She'd thought he'd like the new her. She closed her eyes and took deep breaths. She knew this would happen, but she'd hoped that any confrontation would come later rather than sooner.

Taking a deep breath, Amanda let her words rush out. "My aunt. She cast a spell on me. Because of it, I can't control anything I say."

"What?"

He didn't believe her. She gave an apologetic shrug. He thought this was all a big joke. Well, she wasn't laughing. "I said—"

"I heard what you said. If you don't want to answer me, just say so," Mark said. "Don't expect me to believe something like that."

"I didn't believe it myself at first. I kept hoping that it was a bad dream. But each time someone asks me anything, the urge to talk hits me," Amanda explained, impatiently swatting a stray curl off her face.

"*What* hits you?"

"Haven't you been listening? I talk, speak, blab, chatter and utter absolutely everything that's in my head." Mark took a step back. "You get the idea now? It's the spell."

"Let me get this straight. If I ask you anything, you'll answer me?"

Amanda looked at the ceiling for help. "That's what I've been telling you." What woman in her right mind would walk around with such a disadvantage? She could tell he still didn't believe her.

Mark chuckled. "Okay Amanda, fun and games are officially over." He shook his head. "Spells. Nice one. You're pulling my leg right?" He shrugged and turned to enter his office.

The unfeeling jerk. He had just brushed her off and dismissed her predicament. Furious, the words flew out of her mouth. Uncontrollable. Unstoppable. Faster and faster, each word picked up momentum, hurtling her life out of control.

"If I was pulling your leg you'd know it because I wouldn't stop there." The last word ended on a squeak. Engulfed in a cold sweat of fear, she stared in mortification at Mark's rigid back.

"I'm out of here." Heart pounding, Amanda charged toward the office door.

Chapter Five

ঌ

"Where do you think you're going?" Mark's hand reached over her head and stopped the door from opening.

"Home." Amanda could hear the hysteria in her voice. "And I'm not coming back 'til this blasted curse is lifted."

Mark cleared his throat. "I—I don't know what to say."

Her burst of laughter held panic and tears. "Hey don't worry. With this spell I'm doing more than enough talking for the both of us." She held onto the doorknob for dear life.

Heart pounding, she could feel the tension from Mark's body radiate into her own already overcharged one. Pulling more than his leg? Oh God, now Mark would think she had lost it. Amanda craved the safety of home, but that was not meant to be.

Mark gently pried her hand off the doorknob and turned her toward him. Instead of meeting his gaze, she concentrated on making circles in the carpet with her pumps, hoping they would open up and swallow her whole.

Mark's astonished voice feathered the hair on top of her head. "You weren't kidding, were you?"

"No." Amanda miserably shook her head. "I wish I was. I have a feeling that by the time this spell is over, I'll have made a lot of enemies."

He gently tilted her chin and stared at her. If it was possible, Mark looked more depressed than she felt.

"Can you get rid of this spell somehow?"

Amanda shook her head regrettably. "I wish. I've already tried reversing the spell but nothing seems to work." Why did he look so upset? She was the one with the overactive mouth.

Amanda couldn't figure out Mark's problem. He'd never noticed her before, so a big mouth and a new suit shouldn't make a difference.

She'd had a miserable weekend, had just made four enemies, her boss thought she was nuts and her mouth wouldn't stop flapping. It was too much to take in. Tears welled in her eyes and rolled down her cheeks as she was suddenly overwhelmed by the torment of the past weeks.

"Hey, it's not all that bad." Mark grabbed a handful of tissues from the box on her desk, thrusting them at her before stepping back. She was stuck with the spell and he was the one who was jumpy. Great. This was just great.

Amanda dried under her eyes so she wouldn't smudge her mascara and blew her nose into the tissues. "That's easy for you to say. I don't believe in magic, but you've heard the things that keep coming out of my mouth."

She could see that the truth was starting to sink in. Still, a shadow of doubt remained in his eyes.

Mark pulled his fingers through his hair, leaving it standing on end. "Could we test this spell out? I'll go easy on you."

"I warn you, if you get too personal, I'll quit."

"Trust me," Mark said with a resigned sigh, waving her forward. "Please, have a seat."

Amanda stiffened. Trust him? Isn't that what the dentist always said before he started drilling? She tapped Mark's chest to emphasize each word. "Listen buster, you overstep your boundaries and I'm out of here!" With false bravado, Amanda marched past a dumbfounded Mark.

Amanda wished that he'd just go to his office. Her heart had started pounding when she'd opened her closet door that morning, and it hadn't slowed down since. She needed to catch her breath and the only way she could do that was if she were left alone.

Her legs were shaking so much that it was a relief to sit down. Mark perched himself on the edge of her desk and crossed his ankles. Amanda immediately felt at a disadvantage. He had a perfect view of her cleavage. Amanda had to stop herself from pulling at her lapels.

"I'd like to go on record by stating that I will not be held accountable for any information obtained in this manner." She stubbornly folded her arms around her midriff.

This only raised her breasts and brought them to Mark's attention. Embarrassed, Amanda dropped her hands back onto her lap.

Uncomfortable, Mark uncrossed and crossed his legs. This was really bad. He should leave her alone, but he couldn't. He wanted the old, efficient Amanda back. And the only way he could get that was to make sure the spell really existed and go from there. He didn't recognize this woman, and it scared the heck out of him.

"I've already agreed to that," he said, determined that if there was a solution, he'd find it. "Just let me know when you're ready."

Amanda gave him an abrupt nod so he could start.

"Okay." He took a deep breath. "We'll start with some easy questions." He wished she'd worn her old clothes instead of this custom-fitted black suit. There wasn't enough of the damn thing and too much of Amanda showing. "Where'd the suit come from and why haven't I seen it before?"

Amanda exhaled. "My sister and aunt bought me a new wardrobe. When I opened my closet this morning, I found all of my old clothes were missing."

"Remind me to send them flowers." Damn, interfering family. If they had kept their noses out of Amanda's life, he wouldn't have this problem on his hands now. Amanda returned his disgruntled stare.

"What else did they buy you?"

"A new makeup case, powders, lotions, perfume and undergarments." Amanda's voice progressively got quieter as she listed the items. Mark had to lean closer to hear.

"What colors?" Mark pulled at his collar. He was in absolute hell. He needed to get his ass off her desk. Yet, the depth of emotions in her eyes enthralled him. He couldn't remember them being so green before.

Amanda's face reddened and the words poured out of her mouth. "Hot red, black, purple and taupe."

Mark could see that she was struggling to keep her words in. He grimaced. "Hell, I'd hate to see the rest of your wardrobe if your sister bought you black and taupe lipstick. You wouldn't wear anything bright red, would you?"

"Yes, I would wear red. And I wasn't talking about my lipstick, you asked me about my bras and thong underwear." Amanda's hands gripped the sides of her chair. "And that's exactly what I have on underneath."

Mark shot off her desk. "Who the hell said anything about bras and thongs?"

"You did." Heat flooded her face under his scrutiny.

"I wasn't asking you about your bras! I was asking about your lipstick."

"Well, next time be more specific."

"Hell." Mark paced the office. "What a mess." He pulled his fingers through his hair as the reality of the situation sank in. "We've got to get rid of this thing somehow." He loosened his tie so that he could breathe better. "God, I don't need this."

"Please! Like I do?"

There was no way he would be able to cope with this Amanda. "Will this spell wear off? It's not like you enjoy having it around, do you?" He sat back down on her desk. This was too much for him.

"Enjoy?" She looked at him like he'd lost his mind. Amanda stood up and stumbled in her haste, forcing her to grab onto his shoulders for support.

He steadied her at her waist. Amanda's body jerked beneath his hands. Inhaling deeply only made it worse. It brought her breasts closer to his chest.

"I have no clue when this damn thing will disappear," Amanda exclaimed, almost knocking him off her desk in her rush to move around him.

Mark trailed her into his office at a safe distance. He rounded his desk and collapsed into his chair.

"Enjoy?" Amanda repeated, as she held files in front of her like a shield. "You've got to be kidding? I terrorized a poor lady on the elevator, and alienated Greg and the receptionists. Up until today, I had no enemies. Think of the damage I can do to the rest of the staff?"

Think of the damage she could cause him. "You're overreacting. We don't see that many people in our office. They're all out on the job sites."

With a desolate shrug, Amanda walked away. Mark stared at her retreating back. Boy, was she upset. She was also absolutely magnificent. The way her eyes flashed and the sensual movements of her body — she was explosive and she didn't even know it. He hated it.

She may have been invisible before, but she was now center stage. She was about to get an overdose of attention from the men in and out of this building. Her newfound personality sparkled with confidence that would set off any man's radar. Mark pulled at his tie again and stared a hole into Amanda.

As though she sensed his attention, Amanda looked up and caught him scowling at her. "Now what?"

Mark raised his hands in his defense. "I didn't say a thing." He immediately got to work. Damn, that suit was something else. And so was Amanda, for that matter. Still, he shouldn't like the new Amanda as much as he did.

This was an absolute damn inconvenience. There had to be some way they could get rid of this spell. He wanted the calm, uninterrupted routine of his office. He just hoped that things couldn't get worse. "Nuts," Mark muttered, glancing toward Amanda.

"Okay, that's it." She got up from her chair and confronted him. "If I find you glaring at me every time I turn around, I'm never going to get any work done."

"Then close the damn door," Mark growled. As soon as the words were out, Mark knew he had been too abrupt with her.

With a stiff upper lip, Amanda decisively reached for the handle. "Satisfied?" she asked, before shutting it in his face.

"Satisfied?" He was having difficulty breathing. "Lady, you've got to be kidding."

An hour later, Mark hadn't done a stitch of work. He just couldn't seem to focus. He squeezed the bunched up muscles at the back of his neck and groaned. What was wrong with him? He should have left well enough alone and minded his own damn business.

Red. Under that body-fitting black suit, Amanda was wearing red. He shifted in his seat and grimaced. He only had himself to blame for the uncomfortable condition he found himself in.

Pushing away from his desk, Mark headed for his office washroom. In the mirror, he saw that his hair was sticking out in every direction. The three top buttons of his silver-gray silk shirt were unbuttoned and he didn't know where the hell his tie was.

Turning on the cold water, he splashed his face and wet his hair back, hoping to cool off. But that didn't help the rest of his body.

He faced his reflection. "Red. Next-to-nothing, red and in all the right places. How the hell am I supposed to accomplish any work around here?" He wet a small towel and placed it on the back of his neck.

Mark debated with his reflection. "I've dozens of women to choose from, why the hell do I keep thinking of Amanda?"

His reflection magically debated right back. "You tell me."

"It's not like she's changed. Underneath those new clothes, she's still the same, simple Amanda."

"Liar."

"So she has a nice body." Mark glared at his grinning reflection.

His reflection chuckled. "Nice? That's what you call nice? I'd get our eyes checked if I were you."

"Maybe she has some bad habits."

His reflection folded its arms across its chest. "Name one."

Mark rubbed his face. "Damn, I'm screwed."

"Buddy, I hope you and me both."

Turning off the faucet, Mark dried off and went searching for his missing tie. He found it beneath his desk. Snatching it off the floor, he wrapped it around his neck, tightened it and nearly choked.

"Of all the stupid, idiotic things to happen!"

Amanda called through the closed door, "Did you say something?"

"Nothing. I was just thinking out loud," Mark called back.

Quickly picking up his suit jacket off the back of his chair, he threw it over his arm, grabbed his briefcase and opened the door. He adjusted his already perfect cuffing so he wouldn't have to look at Amanda. "I'm off to meet with the supervisor on one of our job sites. If you need me, you can reach me on my cell."

Mark slipped on his jacket. "While I'm away, try to contact Mr. Bassett and set up a dinner appointment." Mark flung open the door and waved at Amanda without a backward glance. "Hold that door," he yelled, and dove for the closing elevator.

Amanda banged away at her computer. She had been on pins and needles all morning waiting to see what he would do next. Each time she heard the smallest of sounds she jumped.

Instead, Mark had walked out of there totally unaffected. "Men," she muttered disgustedly.

The phone rang and Amanda snatched it up. "Global Investments."

"Hello Amanda. Perhaps this is a bad time to be calling?"

She recognized the voice. It was one of the headhunters who kept trying to lure her away from her job.

She got straight to the point. "What can I do for you?"

His honeyed voice came over the phone. "You got that all wrong. It's what I can do for you."

"Look, I appreciate your call, but I'm not interested."

The man's persistent voice continued trying to entice Amanda. "I know, but these people want you. You'll double your salary and you'll be managing your own department."

Everything Amanda was working toward. She sighed, but remained adamant. "I'm still not interested."

He finally ran out of patience. "What logical reason could you possibly have for turning down a chance like this?"

The man sounded frustrated, but nothing could compare to what she was feeling. "You want logical? I'll give you logical. How about I'm in love with my boss?" Amanda slammed the phone down and cringed. She was certain that she wouldn't hear from him again.

Amanda pulled her fingers through her hair. She was being torn apart. The men around her were either trying to draw her in one direction or were running the opposite way. She tried to focus on the graph in front of her, when a thought dawned on her.

Mark had never rushed out of their office like that before. Come to think of it, he hadn't even given her the courtesy of looking at her when he spoke.

The more she thought over Mark's peculiar behavior, the larger her grin became. Mark had issued his orders and run out of there as though the seat of his pants was on fire. Beaming, Amanda resumed her typing.

If he wasn't rushing out of the office, he was rushing in. The black suit, shirt and tie he wore today suited his ominous mood. His tie flapped over one shoulder as his morning coffee spurted out of the hole in the lid, spraying his hand with the hot liquid. "Good morning." Mark hurried past Amanda with the intention of closing himself in his office, when he realized that the president of the company was talking to her.

"George, did we have a meeting this morning?" Mark asked, dropping his briefcase and coffee onto his desk. "Give me a moment and I'll be right with you."

George waved Mark away. "Relax, I'm here to see Amanda. I need a favor," George said, smiling down at her. He was a tall, thin man in a custom-made gray suit and tie. His short wavy hair was peppered silver and white.

Mark retraced his steps back to Amanda's desk and chanced a peek at what she was wearing. Dressed in a cream-colored dress with a square neckline, her body was molded by its softness, the material nipping at her waist. The desk blocked the rest of his view. Her face was vanilla soft. The makeup around her eyes made her look mysterious. A rust-colored scarf held her soft cascading curls at the base of her neck.

Mark dragged his eyes away. "Sure, anything."

"Our development team needs Amanda for the week. I know that you're cross-training her and I heard about how sharp her views had been at the architect's meeting. This would be a wonderful opportunity for her."

"That's great. When can she start?" Yes, yes, yes. This was perfect. He could get her out of the office and voilà, no more unnecessary distractions. Hopefully, by the time she came back, she would have gotten rid of the spell.

"Right away," George said.

"I'd love to," Amanda said. Then her face fell. "But I've got meetings scheduled and reports that have to be finalized."

"Not to worry, I'll send Hilda to cover for you. She's a temp that the company uses." George patted Mark on his shoulder and grinned as he told him, "You're in for a treat."

Amanda's eyes filled with mischief and Mark knew why. Hilda Doberman hid a dry, no-nonsense attitude behind a sweet smile. The white-haired woman had the reputation of a drill sergeant.

Mark's smile felt strained. After giving her one last, long stare, he nodded his decision. Better Doberman than Amanda. "You heard the boss," he said, coming around her desk, lifting her purse from beneath it and ushering her toward the door. "Amanda, enjoy your training session. George, just send Hilda over whenever you have the chance."

Mark chuckled. This was perfect. "Amanda, this is a great opportunity for you," he said, already looking forward to a week of peace. No words that would surprise him and make his heart jump. No sexy clothes that would tempt him. He grinned at the side slit in her dress as it opened, showing off a lovely expanse of leg. He was so relieved she was going.

"What's wrong? Do I have a run?" Amanda asked, inspecting her legs.

"No." Mark cleared his throat. "I thought I saw a thumbtack on the floor. You can never be too careful."

"Ah, here's Hilda," George said.

She reminded Mark of a French poodle dressed in a dark navy suit. She carried a large plastic bag and her purse.

"Right on time," George said.

"Of course, what else did you expect?" Small, dark eyes looked Mark over. "I've little time to shape this pup like I did you." She walked past Mark as he shared a good-natured shrug with George.

"Come Amanda." George touched her elbow and led her down the corridor. "I'll introduce you to the rest of the team and come back to see how things are going here."

Mark followed the smooth sway of Amanda's hips until she disappeared. He could still hear George's voice. "You'll be working in the conference room. Nice bunch of guys. Now that I think about it, you'll be the only woman there." Mark could hear George chuckle. "They're in for a lovely surprise."

Mark tightened his fists, reminding himself that this was exactly what he wanted. Breathing space. He strained his ears and heard Amanda's laugh.

Hearing a woman cough discretely, Mark glanced over to the receptionists and found them gawking at him. "Don't you have work to do?" A peal of laughter met his question. No use explaining anything to those two—they would draw their own conclusions.

"Let's get a move on." Hilda's gruff voice broke into his thoughts.

Mark found that she had already unpacked her large bag onto Amanda's desk—a workman's thermos and a container with what looked like gigantic muffins. She was already opening the mail. Things were definitely looking up. She looked adorable. There was no way the rumors he'd heard about her being tough were true.

"Hilda, if you need anything just ask," Mark said, returning to his desk. He lifted his cold coffee to his lips and grimaced.

"Is that your breakfast?" Hilda had followed him into his office with her flask.

"Unfortunately, it is." He eyed the thermos she was unscrewing. "Unless you want to share some of your hot coffee?"

"Give me that." She took the cup from Mark's hand and sniffed the opening. "Irish cream-flavored coffee, triple cream, triple sugar."

"Wow, you're good," he replied, impressed. This week was going to be a pleasure. She already knew how he liked his coffee.

Hilda shook her head and tsked. "This will not do."

Mark watched her carry his cold cup of coffee to the washroom and dump its contents into the sink.

"Bad for your heart. Now this is much better for you. Chicory coffee with soy milk and a drop of honey." She finished pouring and pushed the cup toward him. Mark looked at the steaming brown liquid.

"Go ahead," she said and waved toward his cup. "Try it and tell me what you think."

She looked so sweet that Mark didn't want to hurt her feelings. Raising the cup to his lips, he took a tentative sip and shuddered. "Delicious," he croaked and put the cup back down.

"Good." Hilda went to her desk and returned with a muffin. It resembled a small loaf of bread. "Here you are." She placed it next to his coffee cup. "Now, *that's* a breakfast."

Mark eyed the muffin suspiciously. He picked it up and sniffed it. It didn't smell that good and was as heavy as a brick.

"Go on, eat, eat." Again that sweet smile of encouragement.

Taking a deep breath, Mark bit into the muffin and began to chew — and chew and chew. He smiled back at Hilda. "This is delicious, thank you." Mark took a small sip of his coffee and continued to chomp away. The damn thing wouldn't go down.

marching to his desk, his feet making squishing sounds all the way, "please call the plumber and tell them the toilet isn't working properly."

Hilda stared at him. He could feel his face redden with guilt. She shook her head and tsked, then with her ever-present, motherly smile, grabbed another of her muffins. Like a crown, she placed it on top of the files she was carrying and brought it to him.

"Mrs. Doberman, I've already had a muffin today." Mark pushed it back toward her. He wouldn't know where to put this one. If he threw it out the window, someone would likely get killed.

She pushed it right back. "From the looks of things," she said, pointing to his washroom, "you still need more help." Hilda dropped the files onto his desk and with that annoying smile of hers, went back to her desk.

"Hilda," he asked, "do you have any ideas for the advertising of that last project?"

She looked up at him, clearing her throat. A raised eyebrow accompanied the smile he had come to hate. "They don't pay me to have ideas."

Mark's face heated up. That old bird had just put him in his place with few words and a ridiculous smile. He was absolutely fed up. This was not how he had envisioned his week.

He'd wanted no interruptions, invisibility, ease in finding required materials without having to ask Amanda. Instead, he'd gotten Attila the Hun disguised as Mary Poppins.

Gone were the leisurely discussions. He compared everything that Hilda did to Amanda. Mark had thought if he could get Amanda out of the office, he wouldn't think about her as much. Wrong. His body had gone on full alert trying to catch glimpses of her.

Each time she passed the receptionists, they stopped answering the phones. In the corridor, he could smell a lingering hint of Amanda's distinct perfume. Drawing him, teasing him, letting him know she was near. The tinkle of her laughter would float to his ears, followed by appreciative male chuckles.

Just before calling it quits on Thursday night, Amanda stuck her head through the door. "Hi." Wearing a straight, bright green dress that flared around her knees, Amanda walked in, her loose hair bouncing about her shoulders. "Just checking up on things." She brightened the room just by standing there.

Mark's mood immediately lightened. "Have you completed what you had to do?"

"Yes, I'll be back to my own desk tomorrow morning." Amanda shrugged. "The guys said that I should play hooky since I've earned it."

No way. He needed her here. "So how did it go?"

"It was amazing. The things I learned were challenging and the rest of the group was supportive. They were absolute jewels."

Sure, he could just imagine.

"Well, there's nothing that needs your immediate attention here," Hilda said.

"Then I won't keep you." Amanda gave a wave and walked out of the room, taking the sunshine with her.

Mark ground his teeth. He was ecstatic that at least one of them had had a good week.

Chapter Six

ഇ

Working with a group of men had been an eye-opening experience. For once, the spell had come in handy. Friday morning, Amanda felt absolutely wonderful. With her shoulders straight with confidence, she descended the stairs and made her way toward the kitchen.

At first, she'd been apprehensive being the only woman in the group, but she needn't have worried. They had welcomed her and made her feel like a member of the team. Whistling, she sauntered into the kitchen and found her aunt and sister already having breakfast.

"You look like a Spanish señorita," Aunt Lilly said.

She wore a simple but elegantly cut white pantsuit. "Thanks, guys." She hooked a finger into the loose waistband of her pants and tugged. "I even lost some weight." She prepared her tea and toast and sat at the table.

"Have you had any more run-ins with people at work?" Aunt Lilly asked.

"No, I haven't."

"But what if they ask you something? Won't you answer back?" Sarah asked.

"Sure I will, but I've taken care of that," Amanda answered, continuing to eat her breakfast.

"What did you do, kill them off?" Aunt Lilly asked.

"I haven't disposed of anyone…yet." Amanda smiled at her aunt, who'd been watching *The Sopranos* again. She drank the last of her tea and brought her cup to the sink.

"That's it?" Aunt Lilly asked. "You're just going to get up and leave me in suspense?"

Amanda leaned against the sink. "Uh-huh—to both questions."

Aunt Lilly rapidly stirred her tea. "This is the thanks I get after getting the spell right."

"Or Amanda is teaching you a lesson on how to stay out of other people's business," Sarah said, carrying her cereal bowl to the sink.

"No, that can't be it," Aunt Lilly said.

"We'll see you later," Amanda said, walking out of the kitchen with Sarah.

"Bunch of ingrates," Amanda heard Aunt Lilly grumble.

Amanda got to work in good spirits. Reaching over to the passenger seat, she pulled a Walkman out of her purse and placed the headset over her ears before heading into the building.

There were a couple of familiar faces waiting by the elevator. With a brief smile, Amanda calmly listened to her music, oblivious to any question that may have been directed to her. Once inside the elevator, she watched the numbers climb. Piece of cake.

Strolling off the elevator, Amanda nodded at the receptionists. "Good morning, ladies." When Cindy and Misty glared at her, she realized she had shouted. "Oops, sorry." She'd forgotten about her headset.

"Morning, Mark," Amanda said, removing the Walkman from her head and sitting at her desk.

Mark looked up from his computer and smiled. "Morning Amanda, I'm glad you're back."

Amanda could feel herself blush. That was a first. He used to give her a distracted nod as he worked, now she had his full attention. And it felt great. "Thank you," she replied, his appreciation charging her hungry senses. Maybe she should go away more often.

"I wondered if you'd intended to wear that all day?" he asked, nodding toward the Walkman lying on her desk.

"Nope, it's only a precaution for coming and going to work," she said, switching on the computer.

"You've thought of everything." His smile dimmed into a hopeful stare. "Any luck on figuring out how to get rid of your spell?" Mark asked.

"Not yet, but I'm not giving up," Amanda replied, watching her computer boot up.

"Too bad," Mark said, returning his attention to his screen.

Amanda held her breath and made sure that Mark was focused on his work before slowly slipping her hand into her desk and pulling out a set of earplugs. She placed them in her ears and fluffed up her hair. "Perfect."

Her tension dissolved into confidence. With her hair hiding her ears, he would never notice the earplugs. Grinning at her ingenuous plan, Amanda clicked open files and sent them off to the appropriate departments.

The sound of rapid clicking distracted Mark. Lifting his head, he watched Amanda studiously working away. She was a whirlwind of activity. Always formulating charts for the different departments, analyzing data and making constructive recommendations. She worked at such a fast pace it made most heads spin.

Mark still couldn't get over her positive transformation. When she'd walked into the office this morning, his eyes had glanced over the white pantsuit she wore. It softly molded her slim legs, three-inch side slits exposing trim, tanned ankles.

Through white strappy sandals, he'd spotted red-polished toenails. Blinking once to make sure he was seeing straight, he'd leaned forward in his seat to double-check her feet, but her desk had gotten in the way. He could have sworn he'd seen a toe ring on her baby toe.

Her white tailored shirt had slits in its short sleeves, showing sculpted arms and wrists adorned with a half-dozen bracelets. As her fingers flew across her keyboard the damn bangles jingled together, teasing his senses and heightening his awareness of the fluid movements of her hands.

What was she thinking, coming to work dressed like this? Perfectly tailored, totally professional and absolutely disconcerting.

Mark scribbled circles in the side margins of his notepad. He shouldn't even be noticing these things about his assistant, nor should they bother him.

"Not one bit." He tore off the page, crumbled it into a tight ball and shot it toward the wastebasket, watching it land on the floor.

Worse was her outspokenness. She was utterly delightful. Refreshing. There wasn't a dull moment as he waited to see what she would say next. It was because of his stupid anticipation that he couldn't seem to concentrate on his work. Mark growled his frustration. Her aunt should have minded her own damn business and left well enough alone.

As Amanda adjusted and blossomed under her ridiculous spell, he walked on eggshells. It irked him that he was having more fun watching and listening to her than he'd had with his last string of girlfriends.

Enough was enough—he needed to get back to work. "Amanda do you have the last cost reports?"

She continued to click her mouse.

He raised his voice. "Amanda, I need the cost reports."

Mark frowned when she still didn't answer. The hair on his arms stood on end. If she wasn't answering, did that mean the spell was wearing off?

"Amanda?" he called, louder. He gained the receptionists' attention outside their offices. Mark waved them back to work. "What the hell is she up to now?"

Getting up, Mark walked to her desk and clicked his fingers in front of her face. "Hello? Anybody home?"

Amanda's hands jerked away from her keyboard. "Did you need something?" Her eyes widened as a guilty blush spread across her face.

"The cost reports, may I please have them?" Now that he'd gotten her attention, she kept staring at his lips. Was there something stuck between his teeth? He ran his tongue over them to make sure there wasn't.

"Shorts? You lost your shorts?"

His body stiffened with shock. "Not shorts! Reports! I need the files."

Amanda narrowed her eyes, leaned closer and continued to stare intently at his mouth. "You lost your shorts while what?" Her confused expression melted into crimson stains on her cheeks. "Look, I don't want to know what you did with your shorts."

"What's the matter with you? Can't you hear?" He pointed to his ears in exasperation.

Amanda reached under her hair and pulled out two yellow, moldable Styrofoam plugs. "Can you repeat what you just said?"

"Earplugs?"

"Yes." Her flush deepened.

Mark shook his head and sighed. He had to hand it to her — her schemes were brilliant. "You had earplugs in your ears all this time?"

Amanda nodded. "I wore them as a precaution."

"Against what?"

"Questions."

"Since the underwear incident, I've kept my distance." He could feel a red tinge travel up his neck like an army of fast-moving ants. "And the receptionists are staying out of your way." Mark pointed to the trash can beside her desk. "Out."

With a glare, Amanda threw them into the garbage. "So what was it that you wanted?"

From the determined expression on her face, Mark knew that this wouldn't be the last time Amanda came up with a way to avoid listening. But anything was better than another week of Hilda. "The cost reports, please."

Amanda pulled the file out of the pile on her desk and handed it to him.

"Thank you. And remember, no more tricks," Mark said, returning to his desk.

At her break, Amanda hid small water bottles under her desk. This wasn't another of her tricks. This was a well thought out plan. If she had to hear the questions, it didn't necessarily mean she had to answer them coherently.

It wouldn't be her fault if Mark didn't understand what she was saying. Twisting open one of the bottles, she set it on her desk.

"Short break?" Mark looked up from his computer.

"Yes." Amanda's hand snuck toward her water.

"What would you —"

Before Mark could finish his sentence, Amanda had the bottle to her mouth. Each time Mark opened his mouth, Amanda filled hers. She was so preoccupied synchronizing her drinks with his questions, Amanda didn't realize he was watching her.

"What did you have for breakfast that's made you so thirsty? Bacon?"

Surprised, Amanda spluttered water from her mouth and sprayed her desk and computer screen. "Just tea and toast," she replied, pulling a tissue from its box and wiping the surfaces clean.

With bated breath, Amanda waited for Mark to return his attention back to his computer before reaching under her desk for another bottle.

The trouble with this strategy was she drank more than she had to and ended up feeling bloated. "Oh," she moaned, rubbing her stomach and grimacing in discomfort. "Bother." Amanda pushed her chair back and headed for the washroom.

She did this throughout the morning and when she returned from her umpteenth trip, she found Mark pacing the office. "What's up?"

"That's what I'd like to know. Are you sick?" Mark scrutinized her appearance. Amanda couldn't figure out what he was looking for. She looked down to make sure that she was presentable.

"No, I'm fine," she said, walking past him.

"Are you sure?"

Amanda frowned. "Never felt better."

"But if you were sick, I mean, you'd tell me, right?"

"You'd be the first to know." If he was the first to ask.

"Good. That's good."

Why was he still staring at her? "What's with you?"

His neck and face turned red. "Nothing! A boss can show consideration toward his assistant, you know," he said, storming away.

She was grateful that the rest of the morning passed without incident. Amanda just wished Mark would get over whatever was bothering him and quit sneaking glances at her every time she had to go to the bathroom.

Around lunchtime, a head popped through the doorway. "Where is the love of my life?" Bill, one of the four men she had worked with earlier in the week, filled her doorway with his frame.

"Probably in diapers, chewing on her playpen."

A robust laugh greeted Amanda's response as he strolled into her office. He was a solidly built man with a ready smile, and was a powerhouse when it came to business. But when it came to his eight-month-old daughter he was a marshmallow. And in her book, that made him a great guy.

"Hi, Mark. I've come to kidnap Amanda and take her out for lunch. The rest of the group is waiting downstairs." He grinned down at her, while Mark came to stand by him. "And I'm not supposed to take no for an answer."

"I wasn't going to turn you down," Amanda said.

Bill patted Mark's shoulder good-naturedly. "When can we steal Amanda away from you again?"

"As soon as you ask for me," Amanda jumped in.

"Benedict Arnold," Mark said.

"We'll take her, by hook or by crook. We had a problem and Amanda was dead-on with the solution," said Bill. "Admit it — she's the one who makes you look good."

Mark placed his hand on his chest and pretended to be offended. "I'm not just a pretty face, you know."

"Only your mother would think you had a pretty face," Bill laughed.

Mark gave him a friendly push toward the door. "Bill, get out of here, before I change my mind and keep Amanda."

Amanda glanced at the clock and noticed that it was after twelve. Grabbing her purse, she smiled at Mark. "I'll see you in an hour."

Bill laughed. "Not if we have anything to say about it." He offered Amanda his arm and waved at Mark on their way out.

Two hours later, Amanda returned carrying a bouquet of flowers, followed by Bill. "She's all yours Mark. See you on Monday, Amanda." With a wave, he left.

Amanda laid the flowers on the windowsill, dropped into her chair and carelessly threw her purse under her desk. "They're a great bunch of guys."

Mark was perplexed that the cold tone of her voice didn't match the compliment she had just given. He scratched his forehead with the eraser of his pencil. She'd left in high spirits and returned irritated. He just couldn't figure her out. "If you've got a moment, I'd like to go over some loose ends on one of our job sites," he said.

"I've got plenty of time," Amanda said. She walked into his office, dropped into a chair in front of his desk and crossed her legs. Her foot bounced impatiently as she pointedly stared at him. "Let's get started."

Jeez, what had crawled into her bed and died? With files and pen in hand, she was all business.

While they finalized the closing stages of one building and the grand opening of another, Mark continued to frown at her.

Her face was expressionless, her eyes shooting darts. It couldn't be anything he'd done or said, since he hadn't seen her for most of the week.

"Is the table booked for tonight's dinner with Mr. and Mrs. Bassett?" he asked.

"Yes, it is. We'll be dining at The Annex on Yonge Street. Reservations are for eight o'clock. Are you sure you want me to attend?"

"Of course I do. Why, don't you want to come?"

There was no holding back the truth. "Mrs. Bassett is a bitch. If she says anything to me this time, I won't be able to hold myself back," she warned.

"I'm sure you'll have nothing to worry about with her husband there," Mark said.

Amanda shrugged. "Don't say I didn't warn you. What time should I meet you there?"

Mark signed the document in front of him. "There's no need. I'll pick you up since it's on my way."

"I really don't think you should go to so much trouble."

"Amanda, what is your problem?" he asked, signing the next document with a flourish.

"I don't want you to meet my aunt." There went her mouth.

Mark's head snapped up. "Why?"

"Because she has a big mouth." But nothing compared to her own big trap that wouldn't stop flapping.

"What could she possibly say that could top what I've heard from your lips?"

Tingles built in her mouth and grew into a powerful current as dread ran up her spine. A split second later her words tumbled out. "She keeps asking when I'm going to bring my nice, young man to pay her a visit and I keep telling

Amanda scrunched her nose. "I hate it. It reminds me of someone's warped idea of tic-tac-toe."

A look of disbelief was quickly masked by practiced boredom. "You see, that wasn't so bad." His face closed even further, as if guarding a secret.

"Hold that thought," she said. He couldn't fool her. He didn't like this situation any better than she did. His indifference slipped, and underneath Amanda glimpsed agitated worry as he tried to figure out what was going on in her head.

"Excuse me?" he asked.

"That look." She pointed to his face. "What's it mean? The one that says who the hell are you, and will the real Amanda please stand up."

"It means I can't get over the changes in you. But even with the clothes you used to wear, I caught glimpses of the beautiful woman beneath."

Amanda blushed at his compliment. "How could you tell what was underneath when I was covered from my neck to my knees?"

Mark cleared his throat. "Since we're being honest, I'll let you in on a little secret. If you wear clothes that are one size too big, they have a tendency to gap open in certain places."

Amanda's eyes widened. "Oh my, I never thought of that."

Mark's strained smile looked as painless as a root canal. "Are there any more questions you would like to ask?"

Forbidden thoughts crowded her mind. Each one clambered to escape as horror tightened its grip on her body, making it hard to breathe. Pressure built around her tongue, 'til finally, the words rushed out. "My aunt taught me to be a lady, but lately she's been telling me that if a guy doesn't make the first move, then I should. What would you think of that?"

"Your sweet aunt said that?"

Did that squeaky voice belong to Mark? "Yes." She gripped the files on her lap, turning her knuckles white.

Her body burned with uncomfortable embarrassment as her mouth kept going. She wanted to scream "Shut up!" but her lips formed the words that had been locked in her head for too long. "What would you do if I asked you out? Why *aren't* you someone's 'nice guy'? You have a nice tight end. Do you exercise?"

"Holy crap." Mark shifted in his seat and pulled on his collar.

"Last but not least, I wondered if you were a good kisser."

Amanda slumped in her seat. All her thoughts were out in the open, suspended, never to be retrieved. The air crackled with suppressed energy as neither moved or said a word. Electrocuted. She'd burnt herself to a crisp with each word she had spoken.

The silence was unbearable. Mark finally stood up and headed for the door, about to make a run for it, she guessed.

Baffled, Amanda stood up. "Where are you going?"

The door clicked shut. "Certain things need to be said and I won't take the chance of having anyone eavesdrop on our conversation."

Mark gently took the files and pen out of her death grip and placed them on his desk. Her breath caught when he took her hands in his and brushed his thumbs over her wrists. He kept his expression blank.

"About those questions," Mark said, clearing his throat. "Why don't I start with your first question and work my way down the list?"

She tugged her hands out of his and gave a curt nod. "That's as good a place as any." Thick tension grew and filled the room's four corners.

"If you weren't my assistant, and you asked me out for a drink, my answer would be yes. But because I believe that you don't mix business with pleasure, then I'd have to say no. It's too risky." Mark paused. "I was in a situation that turned sour and I wouldn't try it again. I think we should concentrate on getting rid of this spell and returning things back to normal."

Amanda had no intention of returning to the person she once was. "I see."

Mark plastered a smile on his face. "I'm not supposed to tell you this, but you're up for a promotion. If you get it, we could go for a drink and celebrate."

Happiness that she had reached her goal filled Amanda, along with regret. She knew that once she moved on she would see very little of Mark, unless she passed him in the hallways or attended the same meetings.

Straightening her shoulders, Amanda put on a brave face. "Thank you."

Mark gave her a quick embrace and held her loosely. "Congratulations, you deserve it."

She didn't move for fear that it would break the moment. If this was the only chance she would have to feel his arms embracing her, then she was taking it. Amanda held her breath as Mark's eyes clouded with confusion.

He tentatively pressed his hands to the base of her spine, molding her curves to the length of his body. She willingly leaned in for the light brush of his lips against hers.

"Oh, Amanda." His sigh was filled with regret and indecision while his body told a different story. He slowly lowered his lips to hers, making her heartbeat jump. The touch of his lips ignited a tingle that intensified as the kiss deepened.

Amanda instinctively brushed her body against Mark's, bringing a moan to his lips. With a growl he grasped her hips and stilled her movements. Heat radiated off Mark's chest and seeped into Amanda. She inhaled deeply to stop the ringing in her ears, but the buzzing continued.

The telephone was ringing. Mark detached himself and made a mad dash for it. "Hello? Hi Phil." Distracted, his eyes traveled over Amanda. "I'm sorry, what did you say?" He frowned at the receiver. "Yes, we'll see you tonight at eight," he said and rang off.

Mark straightened the papers on his desk before glancing at her. She clasped and unclasped her cold hands and returned his stare.

"That shouldn't have happened. I only meant to congratulate you. Instead, I stepped over my self-imposed boundaries. You understand that it can't happen again."

"Perfectly." Amanda wanted to run out of there.

He rubbed his hands over his face. "God, what a mess," he mumbled.

Amanda leaned forward and tried to catch what he was saying. "Why are you mumbling?"

He picked up his pen and tapped a steady beat against his desk. The insistent beat vibrated against her frazzled nerves.

"I mumble because sometimes I think out loud. It helps me rationalize through problems I might have."

"So now you consider me one of your problems."

Mark threw his pen onto the desk. "I never said that."

Amanda looked straight at him. "You didn't have to. The guys from the fourth floor loved my changes."

Chapter Seven

❧

Her bedroom looked like a cyclone had hit it.

Clothes were scattered everywhere, shoes littered the floor, underwear spilled out of drawers. She'd tried on most of her wardrobe and now was running late.

The chime of the doorbell sent Amanda into a tizzy. "Oh, hell!"

She pulled her fingers through her hair and got them stuck in her curls. "Ouch, ouch." She couldn't remember ever being so nervous. "Come on, get a grip."

Aunt Lilly and Sarah's hurried footsteps raced each other to the front door. So much for her plans to meet Mark and intercept her aunt.

"Amanda," Aunt Lilly yelled, "there's a cutie-patootie at the door."

This was just great. "Show Mark into the front room and send Sarah up," she called.

Amanda could hear her sister climbing the stairs, as Aunt Lilly led Mark into the front room. Her aunt was talking a mile a minute. Amanda needed to get downstairs fast before her aunt caused any more damage.

Sarah's whistle interrupted Amanda's thoughts. "I know, I know, it's a disaster."

"That too. I was commenting on your taste in men," Sarah said, jiggling her eyebrows up and down. "He's scrumptious."

Amanda kicked a shoe out of her way. "Tell me something I don't know."

"How 'bout he's got Aunt Lilly batting her eyelashes like a young schoolgirl." Sarah folded her arms over her chest and leaned against the doorframe. "And you're so discombobulated that you can't make a simple decision, like what to wear."

"Don't just stand there," Amanda said, pulling Sarah into her room, "come in and give me a hand."

"No wonder you're having fantasies about him. Any woman would," Sarah said.

"You're not making matters better by telling me something I can't help." Amanda pointed to her bed. "Sit."

Sarah pushed a pile of clothes aside and sat down. "What kind of look are you after? The 'blend into the background' look, the 'competent secretary' look, or the 'move out of my way, in your face, honey I've arrived' look?"

"The last one." The sooner Mark got used to the new her, the better.

"Right up my alley." Sarah wiggled her behind up the bed and made herself comfortable against the headboard. "First things first — get rid of that little black number you're wearing."

Amanda stripped down to her bra and underwear again. From downstairs, Mark's burst of laughter caught her attention. "We really need to hurry."

"Now, where's that beige silk slip dress with the three-quarter, chiffon jacket?" Sarah asked, searching the piles of clothes on the bed.

Amanda picked up an outfit off the floor and hung it back in her closet. "It's still in here."

A disgusted look crossed her sister's face. "Well pull it out. It's the best one of the bunch."

Reaching into the back of her closet, Amanda pulled out the outfit. It draped the hanger with its flowing softness. Amanda rotated the hanger, making the light capture specks of gold.

"There's not much to it." Amanda worried her bottom lip. "If I put it on it'll look like I'm wearing next to nothing."

With a hand motion, Sarah waved her closer. "That's the whole point. It leaves everything to the imagination, while hinting at what's beneath." Sarah touched the material and sighed, "Gorgeous."

Amanda caressed the fabric. Her sister was right. It was light as air and smooth as butter.

"But first, you're wearing too much underwear. Get rid of this black set and put on a taupe-colored thong."

Amanda followed her sister's instructions and placed her hands on her slim hips, smiling at her reflection in the mirror. She was unashamed of her new figure.

"Now put on that skin-colored, self-adhesive bra that you have in your drawer."

"Is that what those things are?" Amanda pulled out what looked like two circles from her drawer.

Sarah grinned wickedly. "Aha."

Amanda turned the soft cups from side to side. "How the hell are these supposed to hold me up?"

"Don't worry, they will. Take the cups and position them over your breasts and press the sides to your skin. Those babies work on suction."

Amanda followed her sister's step-by-step instructions. The adhesive felt cool against her skin. "You sound like you've done this before," she said, removing her hands and bouncing up and down.

Amanda looked at her sister. "Are you sure these won't fall off?" she asked, looking down at her breasts and bouncing harder.

"So long as you don't make any sudden moves or lean too far out, you'll be fine."

Amanda's head snapped up. "Oh God! It sounds like you're talking from experience. What happened?" She really didn't need any mishaps.

"It's really quite funny if you think about. I was on the dance floor swaying with my partner. All that gyrating made one of them pop off," Sarah said, laughing at the memory.

"What did you do?" Amanda glanced at her gravity-defying breasts.

Sarah shrugged. "I wouldn't have noticed but my partner kept staring at the front of my top. When I looked down, I noticed that one of the suckers had decided to go on a trip and was about to pop right out of my blouse. I did a slow turn so I could face a wall behind me. I quickly stuck my hand down my top, grabbed the sucker and pressed it back on. Then I turned back and continued dancing as if nothing had happened."

"Maybe I should just stick with the 'blend in the background' look."

"Stop wasting time or Mark will wonder what's keeping you," Sarah said. Before she could chicken out, Sarah fired more instructions her way. "Now throw on the slip dress."

Getting into that slip-of-nothing was easy. She slid her hands through the spaghetti straps and eased the dress over her head. It cascaded around her hips and ended inches above her knees.

Amanda glanced at her sister for support. "I'm not sure about this."

"I am, and you've never looked better. Mark is really going to love this. Now throw the jacket on. It's got long bell-shaped sleeves and long slits up the sides, so you get glimpses of your legs as you walk."

Amanda slipped it on, letting it float around her body and settle about her knees. With each move, the chiffon jacket glittered specks of gold.

"Now sandals and some jewelry. And voilà, we have one hell of a sexy lady for the evening."

Amanda slipped on her open-toe, gold sandals and four circular gold bracelets. Placing her hands on her hips, she gave Sarah a conspiratorial smile. "You know, I feel really wicked just thinking about what I'm not wearing underneath."

"That's the spirit." Sarah hopped off the bed and nudged her toward the door. "Now, where are your glasses?"

"Don't need them, I'm wearing contact lenses."

Sarah's smile grew even wider. "Then get out of here before Aunt Lilly says something we'll both regret."

Amanda hurried down the hallway and listened to her aunt's nonstop chatter coming from the front room. Mark wasn't saying a word. Holding onto the banister, she quickly descended the stairs, ready to haul Mark out of there.

"Sorry to have kept you waiting."

Mark stood up with a ready smile. His grin froze with his first glimpse of her, and then slipped into stunned disbelief. His eyes glanced over her wild cascading curls and widened when they reached her shimmering outfit. He was speechless.

"Damn Amanda, don't you look special," Aunt Lilly gushed, pushing herself off the sofa. "Isn't she something else?" When Mark didn't answer, Aunt Lilly elbowed his arm.

Mark cleared his throat. "She's something else, all right."

"Time to go." Amanda put her arm through Mark's and gently steered him toward the door. "We wouldn't want the Bassetts to wait for us."

"What's the rush?" Aunt Lilly's angelic expression held a devilish twinkle to it.

"I need to get him out of here before you hatch another of your schemes. Mark would be swinging upside down from our chandelier before he realized what you'd done."

"In a moment," Mark said, gently prying Amanda's hand off his arm and clasping one of her aunt's dimpled hands in his. "Aunt Lilly, it's been a pleasure. I understand now where Amanda gets her spunk. Thanks for your suggestion about the spell. I'll see you tomorrow."

Aunt Lilly motioned Mark down to her level. When he bent closer she gave him a light peck on his cheek, and then patted it. "You're a good boy."

Mark's face turned red. Straightening, he touched Amanda's elbow. "Shall we?"

As Mark ushered her through the door, Amanda took a final peek behind her and wished she hadn't. Her aunt was dancing a jig in the entryway. With a thumbs-up sign and a wink, she closed the door. Amanda shivered. That adorable-looking woman was terrifying.

When they reached Mark's black Jaguar, Amanda anxiously tapped her foot on the sidewalk. "What was that all about? You have a date with my aunt tomorrow?"

Without saying a word, Mark helped her into the car before climbing in the driver's side. He sat there in stunned silence, resting his hands on the steering wheel, staring blindly out the window. "I don't believe it."

"What don't you believe?" Warning ripples of alarm erupted within her.

He shook his head, started the motor and drove off. Glancing at her, Mark continued to shake his head. "You *did* warn me." His laugh held disbelief.

Amanda snapped her seat belt in place and clasped her hands on her lap to stop them from shaking. "Tell me what my aunt said now."

Mark's grin grew wider. "You warned me about her, but I didn't expect to get bushwhacked. She's absolutely adorable—sweet and the best con artist I've ever met." He slapped his steering wheel and laughed. "I thought my mother was good, but that old cookie could teach her a thing or two."

Amanda's insides churned. Her aunt had gotten a hold of Mark and in her usual, over-ambitious manner, had said things she shouldn't have. "I'm so glad you're taking this all in stride."

"That woman is one smooth talker. One minute we were discussing how to get rid of your spell and the next minute, I had invited your family to a barbecue tomorrow so that I could look over the book."

"What? How did that happen?" Amanda asked, shaking her head in disbelief. Mark must not have been thinking straight. "Couldn't you have just asked to see the stupid book? And since when did you start calling her 'Aunt Lilly'?"

"I did ask if I could see the book the spell was written in. She said that she couldn't remember where she put it and that it would take too long to look for it." Mark idled at a red light.

Amanda snorted. "Like I believe that." Her aunt knew exactly where everything was, from the hidden TV remote to her secret stash of chocolates.

"I haven't got a clue how your aunt maneuvered the situation. As soon as I walked through your door, she told me to call her Aunt Lilly, then steamrolled me with a whole bunch of questions."

"Didn't I tell you to pay no attention to anything my aunt said?" Heat traveled up her neck and warmed her cheeks. "You were supposed to convince her that you weren't my young man, not get yourself adopted."

"I did bring it up," he said, shooting into traffic. "I explained that I wasn't your young man."

"And?"

"She told me to quit talking utter nonsense. That a man with my intelligence should be able to see a good thing when it's right in front of his eyes."

Mark drummed his fingers against the steering wheel. Judging from his apprehensive glances, things were only going to get worse.

Amanda took a deep breath and grabbed the bull by the horns. "Out with it." She might as well get over the worst of her aunt's outrageousness and try to enjoy what she hoped would be a pleasant evening.

"Your aunt said I better hurry up and jump your bones because she wanted a grandniece or grandnephew she could spoil. If I wasn't up to the job, she'd find another candidate."

An atomic bomb exploded inside her body. "She did what?" Amanda shot forward in her seat and the belt snapped her back. "What did she do, put in an order?" Amanda asked, covering her face and moaning.

"She wouldn't let me get a word in edgewise. That's never happened to me before. One minute I was introducing myself and the next, I had the rest of my life mapped out for me. It's really quite funny, if you stop and think about it."

Amanda dropped her hands back into her lap and wished that Mark would stop shaking his head that way. "Please tell me there isn't any more."

"I wish. She wanted to know if I appreciated how well we work together," Mark said, giving her a sincere smile. "Which I do. I may not have said it in the past, but I couldn't have done half the amount of work without you." Mark's cheeks darkened. "Last, but not least, she wanted to know if I was blind or gay."

Amanda rubbed the side of her eye, which was twitching. "Just shoot me. Why didn't you just give her one of your cold stares? I'll bet she's already hatching something." When she got back home, she would have to have a long talk with her aunt.

"Your aunt could pass as Hilda's twin. Both hide an iniquitous sense of humor under a sweet exterior."

"You got that right. She used that nice old lady look and steamrolled you." Amanda couldn't figure out why Mark was enjoying this so much. He might think this was all a joke, but she wasn't laughing. Humiliation and horror had permanently taken residence in the depths of her body and not even an exorcist could remove them. This spell had seized her life, along with her mouth, and made them spiral out of control.

Mark pulled up in front of the restaurant. "She wouldn't be the first woman in history to use what she's got to get what she wants," he reasoned.

"And you wouldn't be the last man to use it to his advantage," Amanda said.

"Touché. Look, I can't be logical in a situation that is totally irrational." Mark opened his door. "Let's go, we could both use a stiff drink."

Entering the restaurant, they were escorted past golden, textured walls that provided a welcoming and romantic ambiance. Dark green ceilings mutedly glowed with dim lighting. The intimate atmosphere embraced well-placed tables covered in white damask cloths and set with high-backed thrones, while touches of wrought iron lent it a medieval character.

The warmth from Mark's light touch scorched her waist through the thin fabric of her dress. A quiver caressed her body, making her aware of the smooth movement of his body as they made their way to their table.

"Madame." The waiter pulled out a large, green velvet-upholstered chair for her. Sitting down, Amanda bent over and dropped her purse beside her seat. When it started to tip over she quickly leaned forward and straightened it again.

Pulling in his chair, Mark frowned at the floor. "There's a candy dish beside your chair. Waiter," Mark called, signaling for attention before leaning over to pick up the dish.

Amanda looked to her right to see what Mark was picking up, but his body blocked her view.

"Sir?" the waiter asked.

"I found this under our chairs. What the hell?" He shook his hand, palm down, apparently trying to dislodge the object. "This thing is like a suction cup." He finally turned his palm up and Amanda gasped.

Mark jerked in his seat, alarmed. "Jeez."

"Give me that!" Humiliation of atomic bomb proportion skyrocketed through the roof of her head as she yanked the adhesive cup off Mark's hand, making a loud sucking sound. "I knew I should have stayed home."

Mark gaped at Amanda's quick reflexes. Her blood drained out of her face, only to rush back in. She hid her shaking hands beneath the tablecloth and prayed that the floor would open up and eat her.

"Sorry, my mistake," Mark said to the waiter with a dismissive nod. The waiter gave Amanda a suspicious glance before leaving.

Amanda glanced down at herself and cringed. "Oh God."

"What's the matter?"

"I just lost half of my bra," her mouth rambled uncontrollably. "And now one side is higher than the other." Slowly, her hand came out from underneath the table, holding the soft, circular cup.

An electric current zapped Mark's backbone as his eyebrows disappeared beneath his hairline. "That's your *what*?" People from the nearby tables turned to look at them. Mark was having a hard time trying not to look at her chest. "Do you want to go to the bathroom and straighten up?"

"I can't," Amanda fiercely whispered.

"Why not?" He kept his face blank as a riot of emotions charged through his body. He could see that Amanda was already distraught with the situation, and he didn't want to make it worse.

Through clenched teeth she answered, "Because people will notice that one side is saluting while the other is at half-mast."

"Oh, God." Mark's eyes darted to her chest and back to her face. "You can't just sit there. The breasts," his face grew hot, "I mean *Bassetts* will be here any minute." He grabbed his glass of ice water and gulped, getting instant brain freeze. He rubbed his temple 'til the pain passed. If only he could numb the rest of his body.

"I know that, but what am I supposed to do? I can't just stick my hand down my top with so many crowded tables around. They'll think I'm a pervert."

Mark scanned the area. "You're right." He squirmed in his seat and was glad he was sitting down. He had insisted that she attend this dinner and now he could graciously hang himself.

This was terrible. Mark kept glancing at the cup in her hand as though it were a baby alien and she, its mother. A double scotch on the rocks would go down smoothly right about now.

"Any suggestions?" she asked.

Oh, he had ideas, all right. But none of them he would admit to. The only thing he could do was help Amanda straighten herself. "I've got an idea." Mark pulled his chair next to hers.

Amanda leaned away. "You are *not* sticking your hand down my top."

Mark gritted his teeth. "That was not what I was going to do."

"Well, this doesn't look too reassuring."

"At the moment, I can't think of anything else. These thrones are so wide and tall that no one can see around them." Mark wrapped his arms around her shoulders, enclosing her in a loose embrace, using his body to block anyone's view.

Amanda stared at him like he'd lost his mind. "What do you think you're doing?"

"For Pete's sake!" he exclaimed, watching Amanda's lower lip tremble as she returned his glare. "I'm trying to make this look natural. I'll look the other way while you do," Mark waved his free hand about, "whatever it is that you have to do."

As soon as he averted his face, Amanda's elbow poked him in the ribs. "Oof!" His breath rushed out as she sprang into action.

He could just imagine her small hand reaching around her breast, trying to tuck, lift and pat everything back into place. "Hurry up," he said between clenched teeth.

"I'm trying," Amanda growled back as her elbow poked him in the stomach.

Mark shifted in his seat and groaned. Moisture beaded on his upper lip. This was terrible. This was incomprehensible. This was totally hilarious. Mark cleared his throat to disguise the laughter that bubbled up his throat.

It would be pure suicide if he laughed. Not to mention it would destroy the small amount of control Amanda had left since leaving her house.

"Are you done yet?" Mark asked, smoothing down his tie.

"How am I supposed to do this if you keep shaking?"

"Sorry." Mark coughed to camouflage his chuckle. He wiped the sweat from his upper his lip as the heat of a dark flush covered his cheeks. "Now?"

"Not yet," Amanda snapped.

She shifted and squirmed in his arms. How hard could it be to fill one cup with a soft, full breast? "Hurry!"

"There." Her sigh of relief slackened the tension that had gripped him. "All set."

Immediately, he moved his chair back. "That's not going to happen again, is it?" He was having a hard time breathing.

"How should I know? This is the first time I've worn these suckers. Let's hope the adhesive sticks or they'll be popping off again."

That was more information than he needed to know. He dissolved in his seat and extended his legs under the table, only to jerk them back when he touched Amanda.

Amanda felt Mark's leg jolt against hers as he stretched his legs in front of him. She was so engrossed in her embarrassing misery that she missed the approach of their guests.

"There you are, my boy," Mr. Bassett boomed, gaining their attention and that of the surrounding tables.

Mark stood up and shook hands with Mr. Bassett across the table. "Phil," he greeted, before pulling out a chair for Mrs. Bassett.

The couple was in their fifties and well established. Mr. Bassett was a jovial man who carried himself well. Short, silver-gray hair was brushed back, and he had a tall, slim build, dressed impeccably in a silk designer suit. His smiling blue eyes were framed by large bushy eyebrows.

"Amanda, is that you?" Not waiting for her answer, he pulled her to her feet and gave her a hug that lifted her off the floor.

She gasped and took a quick look at her chest to make sure that nothing had popped out of place. "Mr. Bassett, it's so nice to see you again," Amanda said, relieved when her feet touched the floor.

"Why, you look wonderful. Doesn't she, Donna?" Not waiting for his wife's response, he continued, "Where did you put the old Amanda?"

"She's still here," Amanda blushed.

He pointed to Mark. "I bet this fellow knew all along that you were a beauty beneath your work suits."

"Mark never guessed a thing." She was embarrassed with the attention she was attracting.

"Call me Phil." He pulled out Amanda's chair to let her sit back down.

Amanda noticed Mrs. Bassett's reserved smile as she took in her new appearance. She gave the impression of coolness that didn't encourage friendliness. Amanda couldn't figure her out. She had never really been able to. Her husband was so friendly and she was so…not.

Mrs. Bassett was one of those tall, regal beauties that came by her looks naturally. With her Dolce & Gabbana cream suit and designer shoes, her chestnut hair neatly coiffed into a French chignon and makeup professionally applied, she projected a woman of success.

Amanda could see her husband adored her. And yet, Amanda sensed she wasn't a happy woman.

Donna looked around discreetely. "This is a charming place."

"Wait 'til you taste the food," Mark replied, passing Donna and Phil their menus. "I've heard only good things."

"What are you having?" Phil looked at Mark, then back to his menu.

Mark read off his menu. "I'm going to start with the grilled calamari and then I think I'll have the seafood linguine with the white wine and tomato broth."

Phil glanced at Amanda. "How about you?"

"I've decided on the goat cheese and grilled pepper appetizer, followed by the homemade potato gnocchi in cream sauce."

"That sounds lovely." Donna closed her menu and put it down on the table. "I think I'll have the same." She smiled at her husband. "And you, dear?"

"I think I'll have the same appetizer as Amanda," he winked at her, "followed by the roasted Australian rack of lamb." He closed his menu. "We'll worry about dessert later."

While the appetizers were being served, Donna asked, "Amanda, when did this transformation occur?"

Amanda leaned to her side so the waiter could put her appetizer in front of her. "More that a month ago." She waited to see how deep Donna intended to dig in her claws. She had known that this would happen. Now all she could do was play it out.

"What made you decide to make such a change?" Donna asked.

"It was more like a 'who' than a 'what'." Amanda nudged Mark under the table and continued to smile at Donna. She needed help here. Didn't Mark see that this was no ordinary, friendly conversation?

Amanda fisted her napkin on her lap and smiled at the people at the table. She had hoped that such a situation would not arise. Dread continued to escalate and overwhelm her with each calculating stare from Donna. Amanda prayed that she would let the topic drop.

Pretending relaxed pleasure, Amanda ate a roasted pepper and tasted nothing. "Delicious."

Donna raised one of her sculpted eyebrows. "Excuse me? Who did this?"

Amanda nudged Mark harder. Why didn't he say something, or change the subject? "Figuratively speaking, my aunt decided to take things into her own hands and gave me a push in this direction."

Oh God, please make her shut up. Amanda wanted to tell her to please stop the questions and just enjoy her meal. She felt cornered. If the woman kept this up, she would have no choice but to tell her exactly what she thought. And that was exactly what she'd been trying to avoid since Donna had sat down and begun her verbal assault.

"Your aunt must have quite a bit of clout for you to make such a drastic transformation. You were so reserved and quiet before. So what will come next? Perhaps you'll become more open." Donna eyed Amanda's dress with disdain. "With your words that is, so that you'll match your clothes."

That's it. Amanda had had enough. She was torn between wanting to come out fighting and dissolving beneath the table.

With shaking hands, she carefully put down her fork and wiped her mouth on her napkin. The inside of her mouth was ablaze.

"Amanda." Mark shook his head.

"You know I can't help it." There was nothing she could do but settle this friendly discussion and hope that she didn't ruin their evening.

"Honesty, that's exactly what's next." Amanda plastered a pleasant smile on her face that didn't reach her eyes and opened her mouth again. "Oh, and I've always been blunt. But my aunt taught me the difference between staying quiet and being polite."

"Which is?"

You asked for it. "It's really quite simple." Amanda looked Donna straight in the eyes. "Staying quiet means you have nothing to say, while being polite means knowing when not to say anything."

Donna flushed uncomfortably and looked away.

"More wine, Phil?" Mark blurted, grasping the bottle.

"Don't mind if I do." Phil lifted his glass as Mark filled it.

Amanda took a sip of her wine and returned her attention to her artfully arranged appetizer—anywhere but at the people who were seated at the table. *There. Happy now?* Amanda thought. Her body quivered with anger and regret. She hadn't wanted the back talk, the tension that surrounded their table, nor the unwanted attention. None of it.

"Phil, how's your goat cheese?" Mark asking, trying to break the strained silence.

"Excellent," Phil said. "I think these women should pay more attention to their meals, instead of ruining ours."

"Phil!"

Phil laughed. "Sweetheart, I adore you, but sometimes you can really be a pain in the ass." He took another bite of his appetizer.

Donna stabbed one of her grilled peppers and stuck it in her mouth.

Mark let his napkin fall to the floor. "Amanda, did you see where my napkin went?"

"It's right where you deliberately dropped it." Amanda bent down to pick it up.

Mark did the same and whispered under the table, "I have to do something or the night will be ruined. Just follow my lead." Mark stood up and pushed back his chair. "Phil, if you'll excuse us a moment."

Phil half-rose from his seat. "Not at all. Take all the time you want." He sat back down and resumed his eating.

Taking Amanda by the hand, Mark guided her to the front of the restaurant where they couldn't be seen. Before he could open his mouth, Amanda jumped in.

"I told you this would happen." Amanda glared at him.

"I know, I know. Calm down, I'm not blaming you. I just wish you weren't so blunt. And you're sure there's nothing you could do?"

"Not unless I sew my mouth shut," Amanda snorted. "And even that wouldn't work."

She did have a point. The situation infuriated him. But he couldn't blame Amanda for someone else's insolence.

"Why don't you try distracting her?" Amanda asked, swatting a curl from her face.

"I'll do that. This meal is important. Once we get Phil on board, it's full-steam ahead on our next project."

"Let's get something straight here. Phil is no dummy. The reason he wanted this dinner was so that he could reinvest with us. He did quite well on the last land deal he came into. He won't let his wife's ill manners interfere with his decision-making."

Mark pulled his fingers through his hair. "All I'm asking is that you try, and I'll run interference."

"Or I can have someone page me, so you can finish your evening without further interruptions," Amanda suggested.

"I'd prefer that you stay." He clasped her elbow and gave it an encouraging squeeze as he led her back. "I just thought of something."

Amanda pulled her arm away and laughed. "If you think you can outwit this spell, dream on."

"Just work with me. If you don't like what I say you could always let me know."

"You bet I will."

Mark smiled at Phil and Donna as though nothing out of the ordinary had happened and pulled out Amanda's chair.

"Don't mind Amanda. Things at work have been a little stressful and she hasn't been feeling herself lately." Mark casually adjusted his napkin on his lap. "Right?"

"That's one way of putting it." Amanda smiled frostily at Mark and gave him a swift kick under the table.

"Ouch!" Mark cried out in surprise, and bent over to rub his shin.

Amanda smiled back at him. "Your tennis knee must be acting up again. You must have forgotten to take a painkiller before coming to the restaurant." She grabbed the decorative bottle filled with olive oil and sprinkled some of the liquid over her appetizer.

This was not working out like Mark had hoped. They had Phil and Donna's undivided attention. To say that they were intrigued would be putting it mildly.

"Let's see if I got this straight," Phil said, his eyes shining with suppressed mirth. "Mark's knee hurts, and your pain is where, exactly?"

"I have a pain-in-the-ass boss. Otherwise, I don't suffer from any aches or pains. Unless you count my stupid mouth, that's sore from all my talking." Amanda sipped her wine.

Mark gave up. He shook his head in surrender as Phil and Donna chuckled at his expense.

"Oh, dear," Donna said, wiping her mouth on her napkin. "Now wasn't that absolutely delicious. The appetizer, I mean."

Amanda dropped her napkin on the table. "While we wait for our next course, I think I'll visit the ladies' room."

"I'll join you," Donna said. "Gentlemen," they rose to their feet, "if you'll excuse us."

Mark watched Amanda cross the restaurant. "You think it's safe for them to go in together?"

Phil laughed. "If they're not out in ten minutes we'll toss a coin to see who gets the privilege of rescuing the women from themselves."

"I'm sure you're right."

Phil cleared his throat. "On the other hand, you better plan your next strategy. I don't know what you said to that pretty lady under the table. But son, if I were you, I'd be doing some fancy backpedaling because from where I'm sitting, you've just backed yourself into the doghouse."

Boy, did he know it.

Chapter Eight

ಬಿ

"What is your problem?" Amanda confronted Donna as soon as the doors closed. "Is it me, or are you like this with all women?"

Donna gasped and took a step back.

Amanda heaved a tired sigh. "Look, if I've done something wrong then let's clear the air. If I haven't, then don't take whatever is bothering you out on me."

Donna sadly shook her head and looked away to hide the tears that shimmered in her eyes. She took deep breaths to compose herself before saying, "I guess I owe you an apology."

Amanda crossed her arms over her chest. "You think?"

The beginning of admiration shone in Donna's eyes. "I *know* I owe you an apology. I've been going through a rough patch. I haven't found a way to make peace with myself and I've had doubts whether Phil still finds me attractive."

Amanda's eyes rounded. "Are you crazy? The guy adores you."

"Oh, I know he loves me, but sometimes I worry being the wife of a successful man," Donna said, wiping away a stray tear. "You have no idea how many women hit on him."

"Let's get something straight," Amanda said, planting her hands on her hips. "I have *never* hit on your husband."

"I know." Donna blew her nose into a tissue and nodded. "It's just that I get so..." She moved her hands in frustrated circles. "When I walked into the restaurant and saw you, I thought, *here's another one*. You have no idea the lengths to which some women will go to get a rich catch. One woman had the gall to ask Phil if he would have a child with her," Donna finished, blowing her nose.

Amanda handed Donna another clean tissue. "You have nothing to worry about," she soothed, as Donna wiped around her eyes and blew discreet, little sniffles into her tissue. "So stop being so defensive."

"Defensive?" Donna hiccupped. "That's putting it mildly. If I ever came across someone like me, I'd have my boxing gloves on already."

"You're a beautiful woman, and anyone can see just by looking at the two of you how much your husband loves you. Other women don't stand a chance."

"They seem to get younger and prettier all the time. I've let my insecurities cloud my behavior lately. As soon as I saw you tonight, I had to figure out if you were the enemy."

Amanda shook her head. "You have no competition from this corner."

"I know that now. Still, I have doubts if Phil still finds me beautiful."

Amanda could clearly see Donna's insecurity in her distraught eyes. "You've got to be kidding. Have you seen the way he looks at you?"

Donna shook her head. "No. I'm so used to him being attentive that it's become a part of who he is. I guess I've taken his attention for granted," Donna said, throwing the tissue into the trash.

"Well, let me tell you something. That guy out there," Amanda pointed toward the bathroom door, "is crazy about you."

Donna turned a becoming shade of pink. "You think?"

"I know. He doesn't even notice other people when you're with him."

"You know, you are really good for a girl's self-esteem," Donna said, brightening visibly. "You just speak your mind and tell it like it is, don't you?"

Amanda laughed. "Donna, you don't even know the half of it."

"You must think me a real bitch," Donna said.

"I did," Amanda smirked. "But not anymore."

"I shouldn't have taken my problems out on you."

Amanda shrugged her shoulders. "It's already forgotten."

"I'd like to make it up to you and Mark," Donna said. "Would you like to come to our cottage up north for a weekend? I usually go there with company or to paint. And when I can't make it, I let our friends enjoy it."

"Mark and I are not a couple," Amanda said, moving her hands beneath the automated faucet and washing them. She let her hair fall forward to hide her regret.

"I understand." A knowing glint entered Donna's eyes.

Amanda pulled a paper towel from the dispenser and wiped her hands.

"Your work is fast-paced, so it would be a good idea to get away and recharge your batteries every once in a while," Donna said. "After a weekend of painting I feel like a new person."

With a devilish grin, Amanda asked, "What kind of painting do you do? Oil paints? Watercolors? Or body paints?"

"You really grow on a person." Donna hugged Amanda. "I'll get Phil to call the office to set up a weekend."

"Fine by me. But we'd better get back or the men will be wondering if we're still alive," Amanda said.

They left the washroom arm-in-arm. "Now we can enjoy the remainder of dinner. I don't know about you, but I'm starved," Amanda admitted.

"Me too."

Amanda held Mark's stare and walked back confidently. The worst of the evening was over. As a backup Mark had failed abysmally. Donna had kept firing her shots and he'd run for cover. Literally. Ducking under the table had only made her more conscious of her predicament.

She squared her shoulders and knew exactly the picture she made. Each time she passed under a light her dress shimmered, and she sensed other men's eyes following her movements, fantasizing what lay beneath. Her breasts gently bounced with each step. Amanda was amazed that the soft cups were holding.

"We're back," Donna said.

Standing up, Phil kissed her cheek and pulled out his wife's chair. Mark did the same for Amanda.

"Ah, is everything fine?" Mark asked.

"Yes. Why shouldn't it be?" Amanda asked, exchanging a smile with Donna.

"I told you there was nothing to worry about," Phil boasted.

"You know what it's like when two women start talking," Amanda said, spreading her napkin on her lap.

"Really? What did you talk about?" Mark asked.

"How observant men are," Amanda said, grinning as an idea hit her. "Phil, let's see how good you are. I don't want you to turn around or shift your eyes to cheat, and I'm going to ask you a question. Deal?"

"Shoot."

"What's behind you?" Amanda asked.

Donna peeked behind her husband and spotted the blonde eyeing him. She smiled at Amanda's little game.

Phil chuckled. "That's easy. A trolley filled with desserts. I've been trying to figure out which one Donna would pick, so I wouldn't choose the same one. That way I get to try two desserts."

"How do you know Donna will want any dessert? She might already be full," Amanda teased.

"Sure she'll have room for dessert. Donna didn't eat much tonight." Phil wiped his mouth on his napkin. "Too busy talking 'til now."

Amanda and Donna exchanged a smile that relayed a secret I-told-you-so between them.

"Did I miss something?" Phil asked.

Donna bent toward her husband and kissed his cheek. "Nothing, dear. Let's eat. All of a sudden I'm hungry. What about you, Amanda?"

"Starved."

From the relieved look on Mark's face and the smile on Phil's, they were just as happy as she was that the hard part of the evening was over. Amanda figured she'd earned herself two desserts from the trolley.

Hours later, they were amongst the last to be ushered out the restaurant door.

"Donna, it was a pleasure seeing you again." Amanda extended her hand but Donna brushed it aside and gave her a hug instead.

"The pleasure was all mine," she said, patting Amanda's cheek and climbing into her waiting car. With a honk and a wave, Phil and Donna left.

"What a night," Mark exclaimed, helping Amanda into his Jag before driving off. He opened his window, letting the mild night breeze cool his heated skin and relax his tense muscles.

He chanced a glance at Amanda. She was glued to the door, seemingly paying great attention to the passing scenery while quietly lost in her thoughts. The silence was a big change from earlier that evening. Before, he'd wished Amanda would stop talking—now he wanted to know what she was thinking.

Yes, the evening had been uncomfortable, but it had ended well. Phil had committed to becoming a shareholder in their next land development project, Donna had mellowed and Amanda had finally filled her mouth with desserts and said very little.

So what was bothering her? She couldn't possibly be angry with him, could she? Annoyed? Yes. But more than that he couldn't understand.

"Are you planning to jump out as soon as I stop the car?" Mark asked, hoping to break through her thoughts.

"You could say that," Amanda replied without looking in his direction.

Shocked, Mark took a quick peek at her as he drove. "You mad?"

Amanda turned to face him. Shadows of hurt darkened her green eyes. "Not with you. With me."

"Amanda, the dinner wasn't a total write-off. We may have started off on the wrong foot, but by the end of the evening, everything turned out well. So I don't understand how you could be so upset."

Amanda tortured her purse. "You have no idea, do you?"

Mark frowned. "Not a clue." He'd been on pins and needles since Amanda had walked into her front room. Tired and irritated, he just wanted her to cut to the chase. "Since you're so good at telling people what's on your mind, why don't you just spill it?"

Amanda gasped.

As soon as he said the words, Mark knew he had hit below the belt. "I'm sorry, I shouldn't have said that." He seemed to only cause more trouble. Amanda's hands shook as she twisted her evening purse.

Mark took his hand off the steering wheel and eased the grip of her fist. "I'm not blaming you for what happened, and neither should you."

"I wish Donna hadn't been so rude at the beginning of the evening."

"Never mind, I thought you had spunk, and so did Phil. Each time she opened her mouth, you came back with your two cents' worth."

"You keep forgetting one small important item in this fiasco," Amanda said sadly, shaking her head.

"And what's that?"

"That I had no choice."

Her soft-spoken words hit his heart like heavy stones. She said each word slowly, getting the message across at how frustrated she felt. She slumped back into her seat and raised her hands in a gesture that said she had had enough.

Amanda's pain and humiliation radiated in rolling waves against Mark's strained nerves for the remainder of their silent journey. Reaching her house, he turned off the engine and faced her. "I acted like a complete jackass."

She gave a tired sigh. "I'd hoped that the spell would take a break tonight. Wishful thinking I guess."

The level of Amanda's distress was high. She still faced forward and held herself rigidly. He'd never seen Amanda so upset before.

"See you at the office on Monday," Amanda said, reaching for her door handle.

"Wait." Mark leaned over, grasped her wrist and stopped her from getting out.

Amanda stiffened beneath his hold. "Mark, it's really been a long night," she said, her voice hollow, her face pale.

"Amanda, please listen to me." After the facts sank into his thick skull, Mark felt miserable. He needed to heal the pain he saw. Besides the self-adhesive bra incident—which he had to admit had turned him on—she hadn't done anything wrong.

"I'll see you at work," Amanda said again, opening the door and planting her feet on the ground. Mark pulled her back into the car before she could make her escape and reached over to close the door. Then he put the safety lock on, so she couldn't open it again.

"You rat. Open this door," Amanda demanded, rattling the handle. She pushed the curls away from her face and glared at him. "*Kindly* open this door," she said through clenched teeth.

"Not until you listen to me."

"Then talk." She crossed her arms over her chest.

"I've never known you to run away from a challenge and that's what this spell is—a challenge. Besides, I'll be here tomorrow morning to collect the three of you for the barbecue. You should either forget what happened tonight, or brush up on your acting and lip-synching."

"Shit." Amanda squeezed her eyes shut and pinched the bridge of her nose. "I don't think that's a good idea. I'll make an excuse to my aunt and sister why you couldn't make it."

"I know that you're afraid of humiliating yourself in front of my family. But hiding won't solve anything. Tomorrow the spell will still be here, waiting to ambush your mouth and any people you come into contact with."

"Then you should understand that going to your barbeque is the last thing I intend to do."

"The invitation still stands," Mark firmly said.

"Look, right now is not a good time to be discussing this."

"Neither is tomorrow morning. You'd have to break the news to them at the last minute and it would upset your aunt. She was really looking forward to it." He was playing dirty, appealing to Amanda's tender spot for her aunt. He already felt like a heel, so what was a little more gentle persuasion going to hurt? "Besides, your aunt is a smart cookie. As soon as you tell her I'm not going to show up she's going to ask you questions that will force you to tell the truth."

"Don't you think I know that?"

"What if we compromise? You come tomorrow and I'll try to keep everyone away from you at the barbeque," Mark suggested, watching Amanda weaken. "We can even work on the spell."

"Won't your family think it odd?"

"No, they'll just think I'm keeping you near me to make you feel comfortable."

"And what about the spell?"

Mark shrugged. "I'll take you somewhere private, where no one can see or hear what we're doing and make things more awkward for you." He didn't care what anyone thought, so long as Amanda felt better about herself.

"Well…I suppose that way I won't have to worry about devising any last minute tricks to avoid talking."

"Speaking of tricks, that's another thing I've been curious about," Mark said.

The dashboard lights illuminated Amanda, making her look like a golden angel as she leaned her head against the headrest. "What things?"

"I know about the Walkman and the earplugs. What else did you do?"

"Every time I thought you might ask me a question I was worried about, I drank water. That way I could mumble into the bottle."

"Go on."

"But I drank so much, that I spent most of the day going back and forth to the washroom."

"That finally makes sense," Mark said, shifting his weight and moving closer. "You really had me worried. I thought you were sick, and it upset me that you didn't feel you could confide in me." His second thought had been that she was pregnant, which was none of his damn business.

"I wasn't."

"I'm starting to understand some of your peculiar behaviors lately," Mark smiled. "You can't begin to comprehend the things I've thought these last few weeks."

"Sounds like you've had a rough time. I guess you were shocked when you learned about the spell, but nothing can compare to the hell I've been through."

"You might think so, but put yourself in my shoes. One," Mark ticked off his fingers as he summarized the list, "I thought you were losing your hearing," he raised another finger, "two, that you had a toothache and couldn't speak," a third finger joined the second, "and finally, that you were sick."

Amanda finally chuckled. While she had been handling her own circumstances, Mark had had to deal with the repercussions of her misinterpreted actions.

"Let's just say that, all in all, it hasn't been your average month," Mark said, slumping back in his seat.

"No, it hasn't."

"If we work on the spell together, perhaps we could break it," Mark suggested, wrapping a curl behind her ear.

The air thickened with tension. Taking deep breaths, Amanda tried to steady her nerves. "I'm counting on that."

Mark smiled. "You see, I do come up with some pretty good ideas."

"This one's not bad, but the one you made back at the restaurant about playing along was."

"At least I'm trying. Am I the only one giving you bad suggestions?" Mark relaxed in his seat.

Her mouth began to tingle. She closed her eyes and let her words fly out of her mouth. "No, my aunt gave me the most horrible advice when she told me that if a guy didn't make the first move, I should jump his bones. But you already know that."

"Your sweet aunt has a habit of distributing that recommendation around," Mark replied, drumming his fingers against the steering wheel before turning to her.

"What are you doing?" Amanda took a deep breath and tried to relax.

"Thinking," Mark replied, dragging his fingers through his hair. "This spell has really complicated things. I liked my life just the way it was."

"Well, I didn't," Amanda stated, stubbornly raising her chin. "I like the new me better. Well, the clothes I love. The annoying habit of speaking when I don't want to, not so much. But the least you can do is show a little more compassion."

"Damn it, Amanda, I've tried sympathizing with your situation, what more do you want me to do?"

"Kiss me." Her private thoughts shot out like a bullet from a handgun—too fast to stop and lethal enough to leave a trail of destruction.

The blood drained from Mark's face, leaving Amanda staring at two blue orbs filled with alarm. A cold knot formed in the pit of her stomach as the tension in the car thickened. "Now would be a good time to unlock the door," she said.

"Amanda..." Mark began, his body stiffened with shock.

"Just forget I even said that. If it weren't for this spell you wouldn't know squat about the thoughts in my head." Mortified, Amanda didn't know where to look. She finally built up her courage to look at him and found him quietly waiting. "You said it yourself, it's only natural to be curious."

His eyes filled with embarrassed regret. Amanda knew he didn't return her feelings, but the reality felt worse than she had expected. He didn't want to hurt her, but at the same time, Amanda knew she had no place in his life other than as his assistant.

Being trapped within the confines of Mark's car only made it worse. She kept a brave face while the rest of her crumbled. What had she expected? He hadn't shown any interest before, so what made her think a new wardrobe and attitude would catch his attention?

Mark gently took Amanda's hands in his. Her breath caught when his thumbs brushed over her wrists. "Amanda, I've tried office relationships and they don't work. I've been in a situation that turned bad and I won't do it again. I think we should concentrate on getting rid of this spell and returning things to normal."

Her sorrow seemed to weigh her down. "I understand."

She held her breath and didn't move as he hugged her awkwardly, fearful of breaking the moment.

Like driving on an oil-slicked mountainous road, Amanda drew closer to the edge, closer to Mark, and waited for the Earth to crumble beneath her feet. Her breath whooshed out of her lungs when Mark caressed the side of her face.

Slowly, he raised his other hand and cupped her face. "Hell," he sighed, brushing his lips against hers. "I knew this would happen." He captured her lips and deepened the kiss.

Her heart skidded to a stop then charged forward. Her dreams hadn't come close to the beauty of his touch. Amanda ran her hands up his chest, and let the warmth of his body seep into her cold fingers.

His hands moved the flimsy material of her jacket out of his way, so that he could wrap his fingers around her waist and draw her closer. His lips ignited a tingle that intensified and consumed her. Tilting her head back, he nibbled at her lips and brushed his tongue along their seam. His groan fanned her need for more.

Mark adjusted his body to hers and banged his knee against the gears. "Damn!" Inhaling deeply, he rested his forehead against hers. His chest rose and fell with each deep breath he took. "I'm sorry. That shouldn't have happened."

Amanda pulled away and let reality intrude. "Stop apologizing, I asked for it."

"It still doesn't make it right."

"I understand," she said with a weary sigh. "I've really had enough for one night." She heard the release of the lock and got out of the car, closing the door behind her. With her remaining energy, she made her way to the illuminated porch.

"Amanda?" Mark called out his open window.

She could hear shades of regret and remorse in his voice. "Whatever you want to tell me can wait until tomorrow," Amanda called over her shoulder, and kept on walking.

She closed the door behind her and leaned against it, listening to the sound of Mark's departing car. "That was memorable," Amanda said sarcastically, feeling bruised from the inside out.

"Well I should say so. With all the smooching I saw, that car could run without fuel." Aunt Lilly's voice drifted from the shadows of the dark front room.

"It's not what you think."

She was too tired to get mad at her aunt for snooping. When she didn't return her aunt's smile, Aunt Lilly's happiness faded from her eyes. "Oh Amanda, I'm sorry." She reached out to pat her arm.

"You're the third person to apologize tonight."

"Oh dear, it's that way is it? I thought I had witnessed a new beginning's kiss. By the look of you it was more of a kiss off," Aunt Lilly said, climbing a step so that she could be at Amanda's eye level.

"Something like that."

With a nod filled with compassion, Aunt Lilly stomped up the stairs. "That boy's got rocks in his head."

Amanda smiled sadly at her aunt's retreating backside.

She dragged her feet to the stairs. Taking the first step, Amanda noticed that the kitchen light was still on. Sighing, she headed down the hall. About to switch off the lights, Amanda found Sarah sitting at the table nursing a cup of tea. "Hi, there."

"Hey yourself."

"You okay?"

"Couldn't be better," Sarah said, valiantly attempting to cover her morose expression with a smile. "Why are you home so early? I figured with the way the evening started you'd be calling in to tell me you weren't coming home until tomorrow morning."

Amanda pulled out the seat next to her sister. "Oh, it started off with a bang when one of the cups holding my breasts decided to pop off, and ended with an explosion when Mark said that he never mixes business with pleasure." She leaned her elbows on the kitchen table and covered her face with her hands.

"You've had a horrible evening."

Amanda dropped her hands onto the table. "Let's just say that I'm really getting tired of this spell." She wanted control over her new life and to keep the strides she'd made. She wasn't going to trade in all the hard-earned advances just to return to a person she no longer recognized.

Sarah stirred her tea. "I'm sorry you're going through so much."

Amanda shrugged. "It's not your fault I'm in this predicament," Amanda replied, scrutinizing her sister. She reminded her of a cat, licking her wounds in private. "Anyway, I know why *I'm* up late and depressed, but why are you?"

"I couldn't sleep, so I came down and made myself a cup of tea." Sarah pushed her teacup away.

"Since when can't you sleep? You're the one who can fall asleep standing up. Fess up. It's only fair that you share your problems when you know so many of mine."

Sarah took a deep breath. "I got into a little accident."

"Are you hurt?" Amanda asked anxiously, taking in her sister's pallor.

Sarah shook her head. "No."

"So what happened?"

"After you'd left, I remembered that I had to collect the accounting programs from Dr. Abraham's office, so I rushed over there. After I picked up my work, I was in such a hurry to get back. I checked my rearview mirror to see if the space behind me was empty and it was. But when I started to back out a car pulled into the spot behind me and I didn't notice until it was too late."

"Oh Lord, you hit the other car."

Sarah nodded. "That's not the worst of it."

"Did anyone get hurt? Was there a lot of damage?"

"No one got hurt and the bumper was only scratched."

"I don't get it. Why are you so miserable if everything turned out okay?" Amanda asked.

"Because I backed into one of my ex-boyfriends."

Amanda's mouth dropped open. Just by her sister's expression, Amanda knew which one it was. "Anthony?"

"Yup. One and the same. He still looks good, by the way," Sarah added.

"I wouldn't know, because I never got the chance to meet the guy."

Sarah raised her hands. "Don't even go there."

"I'm so sorry, Sarah."

Sarah shrugged. "It doesn't matter anymore. It's water under the bridge now."

She couldn't fool Amanda. Out of all the men she had dated, Anthony had meant—and hurt her—the most. If Amanda ever had the chance to meet the guy, she'd let him have it. "So after you saw there was no damage, you went your separate ways?"

"Not exactly." Sarah visibly cringed. "You see, he had his grandmother in the passenger seat, or I think that's who it was since I never got to meet her. Anyway, he was so upset that she might be hurt that he waved his hands at me and ranted in Italian."

"And what did you do? Or shouldn't I ask?"

Sarah blushed. "I yelled right back."

Amanda shook her head in sympathy. "Oh, Sarah."

Desperate times like this called for desperate measures. And nothing soothed better than ice cream. Amanda opened the freezer and took out two liters—cookie-dough and rocky road. Next, she placed chocolate and butterscotch syrups on the lazy Susan. Sitting down, she reached for two spoons from the ceramic holder on the table.

Amanda passed Sarah a spoon. "Here you go. You know what they say about misery loving company, so dig in."

Ripping off the lid of the cookie-dough ice cream, Amanda scooped out a mouthful and poured butterscotch syrup over the spoon, letting the excess fall into the container. Then she spun the lazy Susan so her sister could get to the syrup.

"Here come the pounds I just lost. I should get myself a really baggy sweatshirt that says 'Lost and Found'. No matter what I do to lose these pounds, they always seem to find me," Amanda said drolly.

"You're too much, you know that?" Sarah asked, swirling the lazy Susan so the syrups were back in front of Amanda.

Amanda pointed her spoon at Sarah. "Look on the bright side. Tomorrow at Mark's barbecue you might meet someone special and forget about the jerk altogether," Amanda replied, spinning the syrups back to her sister. "It's his loss for not finding out what a great person you are."

"Has anyone ever told you that you're wonderful for a person's self-esteem?" Sarah asked, returning the syrups once again.

"Someone said those exact words to me tonight." Amanda squeezed more butterscotch syrup over her ice cream. At the rate she was going, she might as well empty the damn bottle.

Chapter Nine

ഌ

"Girls," Amanda could hear her aunt yelling at the stairs, "Mark will be here any minute."

"We're already in the kitchen," Amanda called out, as her sister pushed her soggy cereal from side to side.

"Good morning." Like a tornado bursting with energy and floral prints, her aunt rushed into the kitchen. "My, don't we look nice," she observed, before pouring herself a cup of coffee and joining them at the table.

"Morning," Amanda replied, dipping her teabag into her steaming cup of water.

They may have dressed in summer colors, but Amanda and Sarah's moods better suited a funeral. Her sister looked pretty in a bright green sundress with spaghetti straps and her hair tied back, but Amanda knew that her colorful attire hid a heavy heart.

Amanda wore a short-sleeved, cream-colored shirt, khaki shorts and sneakers, and was drowning the teabag in her cup, wishing she could do the same with her misery.

"Sarah won't be coming, she forgot she had a morning appointment," said Amanda.

"Fiddlesticks," Aunt Lilly said, scrutinizing them.

Before her aunt could ask a question, Amanda pushed a large bag of her favorite cookies in front of her. "Here, have one." That should keep her aunt's mouth occupied, at least for a while.

Aunt Lilly dunked a cookie in her coffee. "How are you?"

Amanda took a bite of her toast. "Could be better."

Aunt Lilly looked from one girl to the other. "You both look like your cats just died."

"We don't have cats," Amanda replied, stirring two heaping teaspoons of sugar into her tea. She needed the boost of energy.

"Wrong pussy," Aunt Lilly said, giving her niece a sarcastic look.

"Please, Aunt Lill!" She couldn't stomach her aunt's crude honesty so early in the morning.

"Your language is worse than a sailor's," Sarah said. "Where'd you learn to talk like that?"

"From the television shows I watch on satellite," Aunt Lilly said.

"We don't have a satellite dish," Amanda pointed out, pushing aside her breakfast as her misgivings about going to the barbeque grew by the minute.

The horror that was last night still held her in a death grip. She rubbed her pounding temples and remembered the things she'd said at dinner and in the car. A kiss. She'd asked him for a kiss. An unwelcome blush crawled up her cheeks just thinking of Mark's shocked expression. But nothing could compare to the mortification she'd felt at his reaction.

"Sure we do," Aunt Lilly contradicted.

Sarah pushed away the coagulated cereal and grimaced. "Since when?"

"A while back." Aunt Lilly cleared her throat, "But we're not talking about my satellite dish. Sarah, you have dark circles under your eyes. And Amanda, last night you were radiant, today you're in a black mood." Aunt Lilly turned her attention back to Amanda. "Do you have something to say?"

"There's plenty to tell but we were hoping that, for once, you wouldn't be a nosy-body," Amanda supplied, hoping that her aunt got the hint.

"Not going to happen," Aunt Lilly stated, clasping her hands over her chest and pointedly staring at her. "Either you tell me what's going on, or I'll start asking questions. And we all know what happens when people ask you questions."

Amanda knew that if she didn't explain, she'd end up saying more than she wanted to about last night's disastrous fiasco.

"The evening started off really well, but there was someone there who wasn't so nice and I told her so. Mark got upset because it was one of our potential investors." Amanda watched her aunt work herself up into a tizzy.

"What is the matter with that boy?"

Amanda felt her lips twitch as they readied themselves to speak. She swallowed some tea to slow her words but they poured out as soon as she swallowed. "Nothing. Mark isn't used to the new me. When he figured out a plan to help the situation it was already too late. And when he finally ran interference, he put his foot in his mouth." Thinking about last night only upset Amanda all over again.

Aunt Lilly dunked another cookie and listened intently. "Go on."

"I also told him that I didn't think it was a good idea to go on this picnic. But he insisted that it would disappoint you."

"Disappoint me? My eye!" Aunt Lilly stuck her hand into the cookie bag and pulled out more. "I'll bet you a month's subscription to my TV guide that he's already trying to figure out a way to make amends."

Sarah snatched a cookie out of her aunt's hand. "And when he does, don't give in too quickly," she said to Amanda, popping the cookie into her mouth.

"That's right," Aunt Lilly agreed, waving a half-dunked cookie around. "Show him some backbone and don't let him see that it bothers you."

"She's right, you know," Sarah said. "I bet people have treated you differently since you started telling them what you thought."

"Yeah, they stay away." Amanda reached for her tea and finished it in one gulp. "So, you still want to go to this barbecue?" she asked her aunt.

"Aye."

"Is there anything I can bribe you with to change your mind? Your favorite chocolate? Dinner at that restaurant you've been talking about?"

"This is more important than food."

Amanda's eyes widened. Her aunt never refused food. "Fine. Now that we know we're going, what are we bringing?" asked Amanda.

"A bottle of wine, potato salad and tiramisù," Aunt Lilly said.

"Did you make the dessert or did you buy it?" Amanda asked, hoping it was the latter.

"Don't you have any faith in my culinary skills?"

"No."

"As a matter of fact, I—" Aunt Lilly was interrupted by the chime of the doorbell. "Ah...here's Mark. Remember, chin up," she advised Amanda, before rising from the table.

Amanda grabbed her aunt's arm and sat her back down. "Where do you think you're going? Finish your coffee. I'll get the door and don't either of you come unless I call. Is that clear?"

Sarah smiled. "As glass."

Amanda pointed at her aunt. "When I get back I expect to find you in that same chair."

She pushed her chair away from the table. If her aunt got to Mark first, Amanda knew that she would swing the first punch. And after failing to back her up last night at dinner, that well-deserved honor was hers.

"Well, I never!" her aunt replied.

"Behave." Amanda rushed out of the kitchen. She nervously straightened her shirt, brushed her hair back and rubbed her moist hands on her shorts. "This is it." Taking a deep breath, she removed all expression from her face and opened the door.

She found Mark pacing on the front porch, choking the ends of a bunch of flowers. He looked delicious, wearing jeans and a T-shirt with the word "Chump" written on it. It brought a smile to Amanda's lips, which she immediately erased. She didn't want any small cracks in her composure.

"Good morning," Amanda said, stepping back and waving him through the door.

"Morning. Where are the others?" He looked down the hallway.

"In the kitchen having breakfast. Would you care for coffee before we leave?"

"No thanks, I've already had my quota for today." He hadn't slept well the night before. By four o'clock, he'd given up on sleep, made himself a pot of coffee and decided to work.

Amanda pointed to his shirt. "Is that an apology or just a description of last night's behavior?"

Ouch, she wasn't letting him off the hook. "Both. The flowers are also a peace offering," he said, handing them over.

"Thank you." Amanda dropped them on the hall table and leaned against the doorframe, obviously waiting to see what he would do, or say, next.

A red wave of embarrassment scorched a path up his neck. He might as well get his groveling over with and salvage what little face he had left. "Look, I know you've had a tough time adjusting to this spell and I haven't made it any easier," he started, adjusting his weight from one foot to the other. "I should have defused the situation last night before it reached the point it did."

"I know."

Mark scratched his head. What was going on? Amanda wasn't yelling, but the way she held herself sent a clear message that she wasn't budging either. Behind her calm, beautiful face, Amanda seemed to be plotting her revenge.

"What am I missing here?" Thanks to the spell, Mark knew there was one sure way of getting to the bottom of things.

As he expected, her mouth activated, letting her pent-up frustration tinge the words that fell out. "I'm upset with myself and annoyed with you," Amanda replied, stepping away from the door and closing it. She walked to the staircase and sat on the third step from the bottom. "I could use a few choice words to describe your attitude last night."

"You could?"

"Yes. Instead, I'll let you use that creative imagination of yours to figure out what I'm thinking. Let's see if you're as good as I am when it comes to telling people what's on your mind."

Damn, she was royally pissed. Amanda had just thrown the same words he'd insulted her with last night back in his face.

Seeing no other way of digging himself out of the hole he seemed to be in, Mark gulped and hoped that it didn't get any deeper. "Fine, how about that I was a jerk last night?"

"You were. But that's just a start, so keep going."

Grudging admiration erased his humiliation. Trouble was, he liked this Amanda more than he should. She had turned the tables on him and he was getting a kick out of it.

If she felt half the discomfort he felt each time she was forced to speak her mind, he could sympathize. It must feel good to hear the words coming out of his mouth, instead of her own.

"I was insensitive to your predicament."

Amanda glanced at her watch. "You're just warming up."

Damn, she was in for her pound of flesh. Thank God he could see cracks forming in her serious façade. He only hoped they meant he was almost finished kicking himself.

"The next time I forget about the spell and behave like an insufferable idiot, and you want to kick me, all you have to do is tell me to bend over." Warm in the face, Mark held his breath and hoped that he was through.

"Bingo!" Amanda's face lit with satisfaction.

Mark chuckled. "You really enjoyed that, didn't you?"

"Yes." She picked up the flowers from the table and inhaled their fragrance. "It feels good to have my thought said by someone else for a change."

Mark laughed. "Before you change your mind, let's gather the rest of our troops and leave. And don't forget the spell."

"I have it right here," Amanda said, reaching for the spell book innocently sitting on the hall table, next to the flowers Mark had given her. Opening to the page her aunt had written on, she passed it to Mark, who read the poem.

"What you think is what you say, for the spell to work this way. Right or wrong, express your right, all your thoughts brought to light. Show the one that you desire, how to light your inner fire. Once everything is said and done, then you'll find your only one."

"This is it?" He flipped the page over to see if there was more. There wasn't. "You mean to tell me that this little...rhyme, caused all your trouble?" Mark snapped the book shut and handed it back to Amanda.

"That, and a bunch of flowers and candles." Amanda hugged the book to her chest. "Let me get Aunt Lilly and we'll be on our way." She grabbed the flowers as she went.

"Is your sister coming?"

"No," Amanda answered over her shoulder as she walked down the hall.

Returning to the kitchen, Amanda dropped the spell book and flowers onto the counter, filled a blue crystal vase with water and arranged the bouquet. "Let's go."

"Finally." Aunt Lilly jumped out of her seat and zipped out of the kitchen.

Amanda didn't bother stopping her and smiled at her sister. "Is that everything?" she asked, nodding to the bottle and plastic containers on the table.

"I'll get the bottle," Sarah said, "while you get the containers."

Amanda picked them up off the table and piled them onto the book, then waited for her sister.

Sarah grinned. "From the look on your face, I'd say that you accomplished what you set out to do."

Amanda shifted things around on the overcrowded table and kept her face hidden. She couldn't get over how laid-back Mark seemed. At work he was a serious professional. Here, Amanda witnessed a man generous with his touch and attention.

Amanda glanced at Mark as he took the plastic container from her aunt and commented on something, making Aunt Lilly chuckle. He was acting totally different from what she had expected. Gone was the serious, hardworking man she knew, in his place was an entertaining individual who went out of his way to amuse her aunt.

It saddened Amanda that Mark hadn't shared this side of himself with her before. What harm would it have done? He had shown her respect, but never this warm attention. Amanda kept a firm grin in place to cover her conflicting emotions.

"Come on, I'll show you where everything is," Mark said, steering them around a group of men throwing horseshoes with one hand and holding cold beers in the other. They crossed the lawn and stopped next to a grouping of lawn chairs beneath some shady maple trees. He pointed toward the pool. "There's a cabana to change into your bathing suits if you want to swim, and over there," he pointed in the opposite direction, "you'll find picnic tables and lounge chairs under the shade."

Hearing someone calling Mark's name, Amanda looked across the crowded lawn. She spotted a little girl racing on chubby legs, her curls bouncing as she torpedoed toward them. A heavyset man chased right behind her.

"Uncle Mark!" The little girl launched herself into Mark's outstretched arms.

"Lia!" He planted a big kiss on her cheek and nuzzled her neck, making her giggle.

Amanda noticed how easily Mark held the little girl in his arms. He was a pro at it. Another stone pelted at her battered heart. He would make a great father, but not to her children.

Her cheekbones were starting to hurt as she continued to hide her anguish. She would never have a part in Mark's life. If it weren't for this spell, she wouldn't even be at this barbecue. To him, she was his assistant. Nothing more, nothing less.

"How old is this darling?" Aunt Lilly asked, caressing the little girl's curls away from her face.

"This miniature monster is my two-year-old," said the man who'd been chasing her, now red-faced, his hands planted on his knees as he tried to catch his breath.

When he straightened, he held out his hand. "Hello, I'm Paul, Mark's older brother. And you must be Amanda. From his description, I'd know you anywhere."

Amanda shook his hand, a small spark of hope ignited in the cold embers of her heart.

Paul slapped his brother on the back. "You're even more beautiful than he described."

The spark leapt into a flame. Amanda's smile turned into a grin. So he thought she was beautiful?

"I explained to my brother that you had recently undergone a drastic transformation," Mark explained hastily, adding, "you look much better now."

Each time her hope took a tentative skip forward, Mark dashed it. Of course he had an answer for everything. She should remember to keep her feet planted on the ground, instead of floating away on insubstantial, silly comments. Everyone had it wrong. Couldn't they see that he felt nothing for her?

"How come only twice?" persisted Eric. "My dad says if you want to be good at something you have to practice. Does that mean you don't kiss good?"

"Well," Paul corrected his son and laughed. "He doesn't kiss well."

"He doesn't?" Eric's bafflement and disappointment mixed into a comical expression as he stared at his uncle. At least his attention was no longer directed at her.

"Will you quit putting ideas that aren't true into my nephew's head?"

"Give me my daughter." Paul's laughter subsided to a chuckle. Holding his daughter in one arm, Paul grabbed Eric's hand with the other. "Come on son, let's leave Uncle Mark to practice." With a wink, Paul strolled away.

"Nice kids," Amanda said, watching Paul drag Eric toward the pool.

"I'm sorry about that. I'd forgotten how inquisitive Eric can be."

"Once you get over the initial shock, they kind of grow on you."

"Yeah, I think I'll keep them. You should see them when they're at their best," said Mark.

"When's that?"

"When they're asleep."

Mark took hold of Amanda's hand. "Let's go. I don't want to come across any more of my family until we've had a crack at the spell."

"Where are we going?" Amanda jogged to keep up with Mark's longer strides.

"We're going somewhere quiet. By the time we get back, knowing how big my brother's mouth is, everyone will think we've been off kissing."

"What! I never said anything about kissing," Amanda said, having a hard time keeping up with his quick gear changes.

"My brother did. And I must admit, every once in a while he comes up with some good ideas." Mark popped the trunk of his car, tucked the spell book beneath one arm and slammed the trunk shut with the other. "We'll use it as an excuse to work on the spell. Let them think what they want."

Amanda's heart fluttered as he again tucked her hand in his. Her body tensed at his slightest touch. She held her breath as he drew closer.

"Amanda?" Mark squeezed her hand, sending an electrical current singing through her. "Do you trust me?"

"Yes, I trust you." But she didn't trust herself. She tilted her head and squinted up at him. "I wouldn't be too optimistic. We've tried to outwit, out-think and out-talk this stupid spell. What makes you think that whatever you do will be successful?"

"The spell has thrown us a challenge that I have no intention of turning down," he said as they began walking again, this time at a faster pace, around the house and toward a secluded forest. "Besides, I always play to win."

Win? This was her life he was talking about, not a poker game.

Chapter Ten

ॐ

Amanda looked back at Mark's laughing family as he continued to guide her toward the woods. "Where did you say we were going?" she asked. Just thinking of the ordeal ahead made apprehension weigh heavily on her chest.

"I didn't."

Mark was in for a rude awakening if he thought he could break the spell. There was nothing he could do or say that they hadn't already thought of to release her from the magic her aunt had cast.

Her next steps led her right into the forest, straight toward her unresolved future. The cool shade immediately embraced her, making her shudder. Insects zipped by, while birds chirped overhead in the lush, green canopy.

She pushed tiny branches out of her way and trampled on the tall grasses in their path. Between the trees, shafts of sunrays revealed dust particles drifting about. She felt exactly like those tiny specks—aimless. Being pushed and lifted against her will by the fickle whim of fate. Without direction, being led who knew where.

The only thing that kept her from running back to the picnic was the warm strength of Mark's hand as he guided her deeper into the forest. Amanda swallowed as she tried to find her voice. "Is it far?"

"You'll see."

Mark's encouraging smile did little to ease her overwhelming feeling of dread. Each step led her deeper into the earth-scented forest, bringing her closer to her destiny.

Her pace and heartbeat quickened as she kept up with Mark's long strides. She took a deep breath and straightened her shoulders. This shouldn't take long. Mark would see that this little experiment was futile and they could quickly return to the barbecue.

"We're here."

Mark dropped her hand and separated the dense leaves before them to emerge into a small clearing surrounded by majestic, towering maples. It resembled a ring of light, filled with wildflowers that swayed on a fragrant breeze. Sun warmed the earth and heated the lavender-scented air. At the clearing's edge, shafts of sunlight rippled on the surface of a shallow stream that trickled over smooth rocks.

"Oh!" Amanda caught her breath. Its beauty and tranquility welcomed her, obliterating her confused world for a moment. "Did you know about this place growing up?"

"Uh-huh. Every time my brother got on my nerves, I'd come here. My mom always knew where to find me." Mark pulled at a tall blade of grass and chewed on its tip.

"What did you do here by yourself?" Amanda asked.

"I'd read, climb trees or pretend to be Robin Hood. I'd laze in the stream. It's shallow, so the sun heats the rocks on the bottom and keeps the water a bearable temperature. Once you get used to it."

"It must feel wonderful." Amanda slipped off her sneakers and waded into the stream. The invigorating feel of the water made her gasp. She adjusted to the temperature within seconds and found it refreshing. "This is amazing." She settled against the grassy edge and let the flow of the water refresh her.

Stretching her legs out and dangling them over the smooth, rocky bottom, Amanda opened and closed them, causing the water to ripple over her thighs, close to her shorts.

Mark sat down beside her and crossed his legs. He rested his hands on top of the spell book in his lap, and waited.

She couldn't postpone the inevitable any longer. "We might as well get this thing over with."

Mark threw the grass blade away. He felt like an ogre. How could Amanda look so miserable when eliminating the spell was what they both wanted? "Let's get to work, then," he said, banging his hand on the book's cover, making Amanda jump.

"Relax. It's not like you're being sentenced to the guillotine."

Her hollow laugh rang about the clearing. "That's not such a bad idea. At least my mouth would finally stop moving."

Hoping to ease her pain, Mark wrapped his arm about her slim shoulders and held her against his chest. "I'm sorry you've gone through so much," he said, his sigh caressed the curls on the top of her head.

"It's not your fault," she replied, his shirt muffling her voice.

Mark closed his eyes and inhaled the heat and sweet smell that was solely Amanda. He was only comforting her in her time of need—otherwise, what logical reason did he have for holding her this long?

Reluctantly, he pulled away and turned the pages 'til he found Aunt Lilly's handwriting. "We're going to get rid of this thing, once and for all. When you look back one day, you'll think it was all a joke."

"If you say so," she said, but her eyes mirrored raw sorrow.

Some joke. No one was laughing. Damn it, he wasn't trying to hurt her, but help. He'd approach this like any problem he had at work. He'd systemically analyze it then come up with an answer.

"Here we go," he said, then began to read. "What you think is what you say, for the spell to work this way." He looked up and smiled. "But we already know that."

"So does everyone else."

He chuckled. God, he loved her sense of humor. When the chips were down, Amanda could make light of her situation and keep fighting. Once the spell was broken, would she revert to the quiet, polite mouse she had been?

Mark grabbed a clump of grass and pulled it by the roots. That was not his concern. Eliminating the spell and guaranteeing his survival were what mattered.

Mark looked back down at the paper. "Right or wrong, express your right, all your thoughts brought to light." Mark scratched his head. "Let's just say that candid doesn't begin to cover your directness."

Amanda hugged her knees to her chest. "You mean my spontaneous, combustible offensiveness."

No, he meant her delightful candidness. The way she blushed each time she revealed her private thoughts. Once the spell was broken he'd never know what she was thinking. Mark strengthened his resolve. At all costs, he needed to move forward.

His peace of mind was at stake. His ethic of never mixing business with pleasure was in jeopardy.

Mark sighed. "Show the one that you desire, how to light your inner fire." Mark stumbled over his words and came to an abrupt halt. Shit, he didn't want to think about Amanda getting it on with someone else.

But that wasn't his problem. His problem was getting rid of the spell and returning things back to normal. It wasn't his fault that her openness had left her exposed and vulnerable. And more desirable.

"Here's the key to your dilemma. You need to find the guy of your dreams," he explained, the words tasting bitter on his tongue. "The solution is simple. You need to date as many men as you can until you find the right one."

Amanda visibly paled at his words. He had made a direct hit on her vulnerability. He plowed forward before he lost his courage. "Once everything is said and done, then you'll find your only one."

Mark's stiff grin hurt his face. "You see? You've been going about this the wrong way. You need a man." He snapped the spell book shut and tossed it on the ground between them. "You're beautiful, bright, funny. Give any man the green light and you'll have them lining up outside your door."

Each word pushed Amanda further away from him and into another man's arms. Mark was convinced that he was doing this for her own good. Judging by her pallor and the way she tried to hide her misery from his probing eyes, this dose of medicine had gone down the wrong way.

He felt like the biggest heel ever. Amanda looked away and composed her expression. He had been brutally blunt, but he needed to finish this, once and for all.

"Who's the man in your life?"

Amanda's head snapped back. "You! You idiot!" Mortification and anger pulsed off her body like an electric current that dazed him.

"Is it about the kiss?" Mark asked, trying to understand where Amanda's emotions originated.

"Are you blind?" Amanda yelled. "It's not about the kiss. It's about you—me—us."

"There *is* no us," Mark quietly emphasized. "You already know that I don't mix business with pleasure."

"If it's business, then why have you talked to your family about me?"

Mark opened his mouth to answer, but Amanda cut him off.

"Don't you think it's strange, you inviting me here?"

"For crying out loud." Mark held back his temper. "That was so we could get rid of the spell."

"Please." Amanda waved his answer away. "We could have done that at my house or even at the office. You wanted me to come today."

"For what reason?" Mark snapped.

"So that everyone could give me their stamp of approval."

"That's ridiculous."

"You think?" Amanda asked sarcastically. "Your father wants to give me tips on how to best you and your brother thinks I'm even more beautiful than you described."

"I only told them of the dramatic changes I saw in you."

"Still, those are not the types of things people say to a person they've never met, especially when that person is supposed to be a business colleague only."

"I only told them the truth."

"Well, you've sent out more mixed signals than a broken satellite." With agitated movements, Amanda pulled her fingers through her hair. "You just don't get it. Forget I even said anything. If it wasn't for this damn spell, you would never have found out about my feelings."

"I'm sorry Amanda," Mark said, keeping his tone firm. "This is for the best." He could imagine what she thought—

he didn't want her and couldn't wait to hand her off to the first available male. He seemed worse than a pimp.

Amanda stood up, brushed off her shorts and slipped her sneakers back on. Who was he trying to kid? He hadn't done this for her, but for himself. She scared the hell out of him. She had every right to be angry at his callous treatment. When Amanda finally spoke, Mark was surprised at how matter-of-fact she sounded, her voice totally devoid of emotion.

"Of course you're right. A couple of the men at the office have asked me out to lunch. I'll start with them." Amanda pivoted around and headed back into the forest.

"Will you slow down?" Mark picked up the spell book and rushed to her side.

"For what?" she asked without stopping.

Damn, that hadn't gone as he had planned. It should have been simple—instead he had hurt her deeply. She held her arms stiffly by her sides, her hands fisted. He didn't know what he could do or say to make a bad situation better.

"I'm hungry, how 'bout you?" Amanda asked, swatting a branch out of her way and continuing to plow forward.

She sounded totally uncaring, but her body said otherwise. She'd erected thick walls around her wounded heart and hung a "no trespassing" sign. He had to admit, when he screwed up, he did it in a big way.

Amanda reached his parents' house and stumbled in her haste to escape him. "Easy." Mark clasped her elbow to stop her from falling. "I didn't mean that you had to start dating right this minute."

She pulled away from his touch. "No time like the present," Amanda replied, waving at Paul. "I'll catch up with you later."

Mark frowned. "You're still my guest. You go have a seat while I get our food." Without waiting for her response, Mark dropped the spell book off at his car and walked away.

Amanda scanned the area and located her aunt talking with an elderly woman. Walking to the first empty picnic table, she grasped its edge for support and let her legs collapse beneath her.

Amanda planted her elbows on the rough grain of the table and held her head. Her life was an absolute mess.

Taking deep breaths, she built armor about her shattered heart. She was filled with deep sorrow that Mark didn't want her and obviously couldn't wait to hand her off so she wouldn't be in his way. She needed to escape this overwhelming ache, escape Mark's carefully composed expression. Escape from her pitiful dream.

"God, what a mess." Racked with pain, Amanda began plotting a course away from Mark. Her hopes for a relationship had turned to dust. She would call a headhunter the first chance she got. She couldn't continue to work with Mark—it would be too painful.

Each time he looked up from his desk she'd wonder what he was thinking about. If he was as uncomfortable as she was, would he spend more and more time away from the office just to escape the tension?

"Is this seat taken?"

Amanda jumped at the man's deep voice. "No." Since she didn't know anyone here, she hadn't expected anyone to approach her.

Her eyes traveled up a pair of muscular legs in tailored, gray pants, over a white silk shirt with sleeves rolled to reveal well-developed arms and stretched over a wide, firm chest. He carried his jacket over his arm while a folded silver tie stuck out of his breast pocket.

"I needed a break from the noise, but if I'm crowding you I'll shove off," he said, his dark brown eyes smiling down at her while a dimple in his right cheek deepened. His long brown hair was tied back and he wore a diamond earring in his right ear.

He simply oozed self-confidence. He was a lady magnet, if Amanda judged by all the hungry stares directed his way. What she couldn't figure out was why he was talking to her. "Have a seat," she said. There was no time like the present to move on.

He chuckled, letting his charming dimple peek at her again. "It's not like the Abbott men to leave a beautiful woman by herself," he said, laying his jacket on the table and sitting down. "I've been here awhile, so I would have noticed you. Who did you come with?"

Amanda nodded to where her aunt was. "With my Aunt Lilly and Mark."

"I understand." His smile turned into a grin.

"It's not what you think. I'm his assistant."

"His loss. Hell, that makes us neighbors. I expanded our offices a couple of months ago on the floor above yours. I've been down to visit Mark, but too late in the day to meet *you* apparently." He played with the diamond in his ear. "So that's your aunt?"

Amanda nodded.

"The lady she's with is my grandmother. I've never heard her laugh so much." He extended his hand. "By the way, I'm Tony."

Amanda placed her hand in his. "Pleased to meet you, I'm Amanda Santorelli." She felt his hand jerk in surprise. His smile seemed to freeze in place.

"Santorelli? There's a big family near here. Any relation?"

"Not that I know of. My parents died when I was young. It's only me, my sister Sarah and Aunt Lilly."

His pallor faded beneath his tan. "I'm sorry, I didn't know."

Amanda stared at him quizzically. How would he, when they'd only just met?

"Is your sister here today?" he asked, scanning the area with the precision of a fighter jet's radar.

"No, she had to work." Amanda heard her aunt's laugh. "They sound like they're having a great time."

Tony turned back to her and chuckled. "They should be. Since my grandmother and I got here they've had a couple large portions of your aunt's tiramisù and have sampled the punch at a steady rate."

Amanda's eyes widened. "The punch has alcohol in it?"

Tony nodded.

"What's wrong with the cake my Aunt Lilly brought?"

"Nothing, it tastes amazing. In fact, that cake has so much kick it would explode if you lit a match near it."

Looking back, Amanda watched her aunt nearly topple from her bench. "They're drunk." People walking by smiled at the women's antics.

"I know." Tony shook his head. "Let them have their fun, they're harmless."

They would have been at any other time, but Amanda didn't need more problems. "Let's hope that Aunt Lilly doesn't get herself, or your poor unsuspecting grandmother, into trouble. She's dangerous when she's sober, lethal in the state she's in."

She couldn't get over how easy it was to talk to Tony. She sized him up. He reminded her of the kind of guys her sister usually dated. Just because Amanda couldn't find happiness didn't mean she couldn't set her sister up.

Amanda scanned the area for Mark and found him close to the end of the food line, piling their two dishes. A small tug on her shirt caught Amanda's attention. When she turned back, she found Eric standing by her side.

"Hi, there," Amanda said, ruffling his hair.

"Hi Uncle Tony." Eric gripped him around his waist while Tony hugged him back.

When he stepped out of Tony's arms, Eric waved Amanda closer. "I need to tell you something," he said, his sweet face filled with worry.

Leaning in, Amanda listened.

"My mom said that I should apologize for the things I asked," he said, holding his hands behind his back and shuffling his feet.

Amanda hugged the boy as she said, "It's already forgotten."

"The last time Uncle Mark brought a lady with him, I didn't like her," Eric revealed with a child's honesty.

"Why? Wasn't she nice?" Judging from the type of women that paraded through the office, Amanda already had a good idea what this woman had been like.

"Well, every time I went near her, she would push me away and tell me not to touch her. She was all dressed up like when Mommy goes to church, and she didn't want to play with me. And if Uncle Mark wasn't near her, her face would scrunch up like this." Eric demonstrated. "Like my little sister when she's hungry or smells gross."

This little guy was adorable. "That's what we call a sourpuss," Amanda said.

Eric shook his head. "No, that's not it. My mommy called her — you know — the B-word."

Caught off guard, Amanda and Tony laughed at Eric's honesty.

"Well, you have nothing to worry about because I'm nothing like her," Amanda said.

"I know you're nice. Grandma says that when a person cares for another person, they do nice things for them."

"How old did you say you were?" Tony asked.

Eric's upturned face stared back with sincerity. "You know I'm seven. But my mommy says I talk too much for my age." He gave an uncaring shrug. "Anyway, now that I apologized, I can have some gelato."

Amanda's radar kicked in. "They have Italian ice cream?"

"Yup, Uncle Tony brings it every year. My favorite is the lemon and chocolate and I stir them together. Awesome!"

"I think I'll try that too," Amanda said.

"You like ice cream?" Tony asked.

"Are you kidding?" Amanda could feel her cheeks warm under Tony's encouraging smile. "My sister and I are addicted to it."

"I have a weakness for Italian ice cream myself. If you want, I could pick you and your sister up sometime next week, and take you to my favorite ice cream parlor," Tony said.

"I'd like that."

Amanda felt a blush travel up her neck and burn her cheeks. She'd only met him, but Tony was a balm to her wounded heart.

"And don't forget to bring some back for me too. See you," Eric said, and with a wave he ran off. "Hey, Uncle Mark."

"Watch it squirt." Mark dodged his nephew and put the plates on the table. "So you finally decided to show up. But you couldn't resist going in to the office first," Mark said to Tony, nodding toward his jacket.

Tony shrugged. "You know me, all work and little play. But I'm glad I took the time to come or I wouldn't have met Amanda. If I had known she was this lovely, I'd have visited your office earlier in the day."

Tony reached over and snatched a phyllo pastry triangle filled with melted cheese and black olives off Mark's plate, popping it into his mouth. "Delicious. But Mark always did have a taste for the finer things in life."

"Go line up like the rest of us suckers," Mark said, sounding more irritated than he should be.

Tony laughed. "That's exactly what I'll do. Amanda," he kissed both of her cheeks, "it was a pleasure meeting you." He hooked his jacket over his shoulder and walked away.

"It's too hot here," Mark said, picking up the plates. "Let's go sit on the lounge chairs in the shade."

Amanda reluctantly stood up. She was uncomfortable with the idea of spending time alone with Mark. To distract herself, Amanda paid close attention to the antics of Mark's family.

"Where would you like to sit?" Mark motioned with his head toward several lounge chairs.

"Anywhere you're not." Amanda covered her mouth. Her eyes widened as her face burned with embarrassment. She remained frozen, staring at Mark's astounded expression.

"Amanda, I understand that you're upset, but you'll get over it. Here," Mark passed her one of the plates, "eat, you'll feel a lot better. You didn't mean what you just said, did you?"

"Yes… no…I don't know." Amanda dropped onto the chair and placed her plate on her lap. "This is really difficult for me."

Mark's chest rose and fell with a resigned sigh. "I'll make it easier for you. If you need anything you'll find me with my brother," he said and walked away.

She glanced everywhere but at Mark. She felt self-conscious sitting by herself. But it would have been worse sitting next to a man she wanted to share so much with, while at the same time, having nothing left to say.

Amanda picked at her plate with little appetite. Giving up, she placed the plate on the chair beside her and for the next hour smiled at anyone passing by, pretending she was having a good time.

Scooting down in her seat, she tried to relax. The group around Mark's table seemed to get bigger each time she glanced over. The majority, Amanda noticed, were women. Mark was having a great time.

If he could be so unaffected, then two could play at that game. He had been honest about his feelings, now she had to move on with hers.

She glanced around to check up on her aunt and found her fast asleep with a straw hat covering her face. Someone must have placed it there to muffle her snoring. Tony's grandmother was beside her, dead to the world.

On one side, Amanda had the soft snores of her aunt and an assortment of babies in their playpens and to the other, the nauseating giggles of women vying for Mark's attention.

She pretended to be relaxed and shot daggers at Mark. An hour of the disgusting display of women one-upping each other was more than she could stomach. "Give me a break," Amanda growled. By the time her aunt finally roused, Amanda had had more than enough.

Rising from her lounge chair, she spotted Mark coming her way. His muscles bunched, filled with energy with each step he took. Her eyes zigzagged across his chest and down the muscles of his thighs encased in jeans.

"Ready for coffee?" Mark clasped his hands behind his back and walked beside her.

"Yes," Amanda replied, looking away.

Mark lined up behind her. "Would you like to try some of the tiramisù your aunt brought?"

"No thanks. But you go right ahead." She poured herself a coffee. Amanda spotted her aunt at one of the picnic tables. "I'll see you later." Perhaps he'd get the hint and visit his family instead of sitting with her.

When she reached the table she noticed that her aunt didn't have any dessert, which was totally unthinkable. "Do you want me to get you something to go with your coffee?"

Aunt Lilly shook her head and moaned.

Mark came over with a plate of tiramisù and sat beside her.

"You don't have to sit with me, you know."

"Not that again. You trying to get rid of me?"

"Yes."

Mark raised an eyebrow and stared back.

"Amanda, I taught you better," Aunt Lilly said, squeezing her eyes tight and rubbing them. "And do talk quieter."

"Don't yell, *non sgridare*," Tony's grandmother whispered.

"Emily, meet my niece, Amanda," Aunt Lilly said.

Emily patted her hand. "Lilly has talked about you and your sister the whole day."

Amanda lowered her voice. "Do you have a headache?"

Both women nodded miserably.

Mark chuckled. "It must be from all the cake and punch you sampled."

"Marco, you talk nonsense," Emily said, squinting at him. "No one gets a headache from eating cake and drinking juice. It's because we stayed out in the sun too long."

"Sorry." Mark took a bite of the tiramisù and choked. Amanda noticed that he held it in his mouth and tried not to swallow. When he finally did, his eyes watered.

"Wasn't that good?" Amanda asked sweetly, sipping her coffee. She would bet that he was feeling the burning sensation of alcohol to the pit of his stomach.

Mark cleared his throat. "I can honestly say that I've never tasted a cake quite like it."

Aunt Lilly tried to smile. "Oh, thank you. I'll make another one so you can enjoy it at home."

Amanda enjoyed Mark's trapped expression. "Oh, no, I wouldn't want to put you through all that trouble."

"No trouble at all, my boy. Speaking of food, Emily suggested that we take a European cruise to enjoy Mediterranean cooking. Now that sounds tempting. No cooking for a week," she said, some of her exuberance returning.

"Aunt Lilly, it sounds wonderful but you've never been abroad before," Amanda said.

"All the more reason to start now. We'll book a cruise for seniors that serves European cuisine. When we get to Italy we'll talk Italian," Aunt Lilly said.

Amanda looked suspiciously at the two happy women. "We?"

"Haven't you been listening?" Aunt Lilly shook her head and grimaced. "Take a bite of Mark's cake, it might clear your hearing."

Mark pushed his dish toward Amanda.

Amanda pushed it back. "No thanks." Her aunt had only met the woman and they were acting like the best of friends. "You should think this over, at least for a couple of days before jumping the gun." If Amanda let her aunt loose on a cruise, the shipping line would never recover from the shock.

Aunt Lilly wouldn't listen. "Oh, we've already decided."

"*La nuova generazione,* the new generation, you think too much. You have to start feeling more with your heart," Emily tapped her chest, "and less with your mind," she finished, touching her head.

"I do," Mark objected.

"Liar, *bugiardone.* You and my Tony are the same. Work, work, work," Emily said.

"That's not true. I'm not as bad as he is. I do have a full life outside the office."

Emily focused on Mark. "*Va bene,* so when were you going to tell me about your *fidanzamento?*"

Mark sat up. "My what? Hang on a sec—doesn't that word mean engagement? Usually you are badgering Tony about settling down and getting married, not me.

Pain washed over Amanda in crashing waves. After the disastrous results of last night, her aunt knew better than to pass such unfounded information. She stared at Aunt Lilly and Emily's encouraging smiles. How could they be so blind?

One minute they had been talking about a spontaneous vacation and the next this half-drunk, adorable lady was asking about their engagement. Maybe she was more sloshed that Amanda had first thought.

"Your engagement," Emily repeated herself.

Amanda looked at Mark then quickly glanced away. She'd already gone through his dismissal once—she couldn't go through it again.

"I like the way this lady thinks," Aunt Lilly said.

Amanda waved at her aunt to be quiet.

Emily pointed at Mark. "In my country when a man is interested in a woman he pays her attention. I see today you did that for Amanda."

"I was being polite."

Did all Italian grandmothers want to see everyone married off, Amanda wondered.

Emily folded her arms over her bosom. "Did you pay attention to the girls your cousins bring today?" She shook her head. "No."

Mark looked cornered. "You're embarrassing Lilly and Amanda."

"Oh, don't mind me none," Aunt Lilly said.

Mark delicately but firmly explained, "Amanda is a wonderful assistant and a friend, end of discussion."

How could a perfectly wonderful day go downhill so fast? With Mark, she was either flying high or digging herself out of a slump. Amanda could sense that Mark had distanced himself.

Across the lawn Paul shouted, "Hey Mark, you have to move your car."

Mark immediately jumped at the opportunity to leave. "I'll come back to collect you," he said and jogged across the lawn.

"How about this? Step two," Amanda said, writing her next point. "If you don't want to go out, then don't. You're not desperate."

"Says who?" Aunt Lilly asked, snatching one of the flowers out of the bouquet and pulling at its petals.

"Says me."

Amanda picked up from where she had left off on her aunt's list. "Step three—in the course of conversation, hint to Mark about something that you want or crave." Amanda dropped the notepad on the table. "Why?"

Her aunt's plan was contrary to what Amanda wanted for the coming weeks. Until she could find a new job, she hoped to say as little as possible and stay out of Mark's way.

"To see if he'll go out of his way to get it. Because a man—any man—if he doesn't give a hoot, won't bother to pick up on your wishes. If he cares, he won't be able to stop himself."

Her poor aunt was delusional. "Step three," Amanda wrote, "stick to business."

Amanda read her aunt's next step and gasped. "What? Now I know that you've lost it." Amanda shook her head. "Step four—leave something around that will gain his attention. I've never left anything at the office and now you want me to leave some personal item just lying around?"

"You're missing the bigger picture here. It could even be a pair of shoes left by your desk. It'll make Mark think of you when he sees them."

Her aunt couldn't fool her. "I know what you're trying to do and I want no part of it. It's not about me moving forward," Amanda said, waving the notepad in front of her aunt's face. "You're still trying to hook Mark."

"That's not it at all. I'm trying to open his eyes so he can see what will slip through his fingers."

redirected with efficiency. It's not your fault that both of you have the same taste in men."

"She's right, you know," Cindy said. "It's not our fault that we both have good taste."

Amanda looked at the ceiling for help. It always dumbfounded her how Cindy's mind worked.

"It's Greg's fault," Misty said.

"So stop pointing fingers at each other. Maybe if Greg got some pointers, he'd know how to treat women properly," Amanda said.

Misty turned to Cindy. "She's right. We'll just have to teach Greg how to get in touch with his sensitive side."

"What do you have in mind?" asked Cindy. "We're not going to get into trouble, are we?"

The evil twins were back. It had been great while the peace lasted.

"You'll see. In the meantime…" Misty picked up the phone and dialed. "Hello, Eduardo? Misty here. I'd like to book two appointments for wash, trim, color…the works. Three-thirty? We'll be there. Ciao," she said and hung up. "Now," her eyes became hooded, "we help Greg get in touch with his sensitive side."

Cindy's eyes shone with excitement. "Uh-oh, this sounds bad. Really bad."

Spotting Greg on his way to his office, Misty called out to him, "Good morning, Greg."

Greg froze in his tracks and stared at them. His face filled with horror as he sprang into action and made his escape.

Amanda suspiciously observed their identical grins. "What are you two up to?"

"We're going to teach Greg a lesson," Cindy said.

Amanda raised her hands. "Pretend I didn't hear a thing. But let me know how it turns out."

"Oh, you'll know," Misty said with a satisfied smile.

Amanda almost felt sorry for the guy. Greg was about to meet his matches and he didn't even know it. She picked up her bouquet. "If you'll excuse me, I've enjoyed our little chat but I'm late."

"Thanks, Amanda."

She acknowledged their gratitude with a backward wave then waltzed into the office with an offhanded, "Good morning," for Mark.

Mark got up from his desk. "You're late," he said, leaning against the doorframe and crossing his arms over his chest.

"I know." Amanda put the flowers in a vase before placing them on her desk and sitting down, pointedly ignored Mark's frown.

"You're never late."

"I know." *Go on, ask,* Amanda thought. *You know you want to.*

"Why?"

Aha. "Because Aunt Lilly needed a ride to Emily's house this morning to plan their trip." She tilted her head, inspecting the position of the flowers, and realized they blocked her view of the doorway. Not satisfied, she grabbed the vase and rolled her chair back toward the window, where she placed the flowers on the windowsill. Taking hold of the edge of her desk, she pulled herself back.

Fascinated, Mark watched Amanda swirl and twist in her seat and maneuver it back to her desk. Her movements made her skirt ride up, exposing a delicious length of silk-covered legs.

He thrust his hands into his pockets. "You look nice this morning," Mark commented, resenting how much he noticed Amanda's appearance.

"Thanks." Amanda dropped her purse under her desk and turned on her computer. He caught a flash of something red and wicked under her blouse as she bent forward.

Mark cleared his throat and looked away. He'd stay on firm ground and stick with business. "Have you met with the individual departments and discussed their forecasts for the next quarter?"

"Already been looked after. Each department's report has been logged onto your computer for your perusal." Amanda's voice was firm, final. "Is there anything else?"

Mark felt like Amanda had punched him in the gut. She looked like she really didn't give a damn. She no longer fought her words and looked amazingly comfortable with the situation.

Move, you idiot. He was torturing himself just looking at her. And still, he didn't budge from their connecting doorway. Talk about a glutton for punishment.

Mark cleared his throat. "I noticed that you've scheduled meetings with accounting and the public relations department. Is there anything you need to go over?"

Amanda shrugged. "Everything has been taken care of."

Mark felt a hot flush creep up his neck and cover his face. "Good, good." *Just move your sorry ass and get to work.* He could see that he wasn't needed here.

"Did you need me for anything?" Amanda asked.

"No, no." Mark straightened. "I've got a couple of phone calls to make myself."

"Before you go, you might as well take these files," Amanda said, leaning over and pulling open the bottom filing cabinet drawer. "I finished them last Friday and forgot to give them to you."

He had a perfect view of Amanda's cleavage. Had her breasts grown? Or was she wearing one of those tight push-up bras? Mark rubbed his hands over his face and tried to breathe.

She was luscious. Her eyes sparkled with self-assurance, while he was totally confused. He didn't know where the new Amanda began and the old Amanda ended. She had lost weight, giving way to deeper curves and sculpted cheekbones. But the changes were more than skin deep.

She passed the files with an aloof expression, which made it difficult for him to gauge her feelings. He wondered how she felt about the discussion they had had at his parents' barbecue. "Amanda, I...ah, I hope you're fine with what we discussed last Saturday?"

Amanda shrugged. "No. But I've decided to move on."

"I'm glad to see you're being levelheaded." He should be happy she was allowing him to remain in the sole capacity of boss. He wasn't. Relieved? Neither. "It won't interfere with our work relationship and we can continue to be friends."

Amanda blew a curl out of her eyes. "If you say so."

Her mocking tone further irritated him. Mark cleared his throat. "Did your aunt comment on the conversation she witnessed?"

"Sure she did," Amanda said, clasping her hands on her lap and relaxing back against her chair. Mark devoured each movement. "She told me the exact same thing you did. That I should go full-steam ahead with my life and I agree totally. So you see, both of you were right."

"Imagine that." His smile felt stiff. He'd opened the door so the competition could walk in. He pulled his hands out of his pockets and straightened his already neat tie. He'd encouraged Amanda to nurture her growing sensual side and now he'd have to watch someone else have the pleasure of her company.

"Yes, my aunt even tried to give me a list of things I could do to help me come out of my shell. So you see — I owe a world of thanks to both of you."

He pulled on his sleeves and fixed his cufflinks so he wouldn't have to watch Amanda. "I see." Mark saw all too well. His inflexible rules had landed him in a no-win situation.

"Great, then that's where we'll start," Amanda said, adjusting her keyboard and reaching for her ringing telephone, dismissing him. "Global Investments. Hi Tony." She smiled into the receiver. "Tomorrow night? That would be lovely. See you then." She hung up and continued to grin at her computer screen as she worked.

Mark pulled his fingers through his hair and returned to his desk. Tony? Tony who? Damned if she wasn't a quick study. He had gotten exactly what he wanted. So why the hell did it bother him so much?

His resentment didn't make sense. He dropped into his seat and opened the file Amanda had given him. He didn't see the words that were printed in front of him. When had he changed his way of thinking? His body had known, but his mind was only now catching up to the realization. Glancing at Amanda, Mark realized that she wasn't the only one who had changed.

Throughout the day, Mark noticed yet another difference in Amanda. She was still the same, self-sufficient assistant he'd always had. They still carried on with their business conversations. But there was an added element of reserve. This was crazy. He shouldn't miss something he hadn't wanted.

That evening, on her way out of the office, Mark heard Amanda mumble, "Goodness, steps one and two completed, and I didn't even lift a finger." He wondered which building site she was referring to.

Tuesday morning, Amanda chose a slim-fitting, red silk dress with cap sleeves to wear to work. It belted at her waist and reached a couple of inches above her knees. It was totally respectable and caressed her soft curves. Strolling to her office, she smoothed the fabric over her hips and straightened the hem. From the corner of her eye, she spotted a man staring at her legs as he walked into a closed door.

Amanda bit back her chuckle and pretended she hadn't noticed the incident. Never in a million years would she have thought she could get that kind of reaction from any man. It lifted her spirits and added confidence to her step.

"Good morning, ladies. I see you're back to normal," Amanda observed, stopping at the receptionists' station. "And by the way, you look great."

"We do, don't we." Misty fluffed her blonde hair.

"And so do you," Cindy said.

They were their own cheering section.

Entering her office, Amanda found an exotic flower arrangement on her desk. She unpinned the card and smiled at its inscription. *To new friendships. See you after work. Tony.*

The sound of the telephone slamming in its cradle startled Amanda. Mark was glaring at her. "What's wrong with you?" she asked, returning his stare.

"Nothing," Mark said then his tone softened. "I see you already have an admirer."

"More like a new friend." She stood in the connecting doorway. "It's your next-door neighbor, Tony."

Mark's eyes widened. "My best friend Tony?"

"Yes."

He rested his elbows on his desk and steepled his fingers. "Amanda, I've known Tony all my life and I feel I should warn you about him."

"You needn't bother. The first time I met him I pegged him for what he was. He's a ladies' man. He wines and dines them. He enjoys the opposite sex's company as much as they enjoy his."

"That's right." Mark's scowl cleared into a smile. "Not only that, he's a workaholic. His business is his life. He's always punctual for all his meetings and never—I mean never—makes it on time to his dates." Mark interlinked his fingers behind his head and relaxed back in his seat, lifting the front legs off the floor.

"And the problem is?"

His chair crashed forward. "I don't want him taking advantage of you."

"Don't worry, he won't."

"Amanda, I wish you'd reconsider," Mark said, running a hand over his face. "Tony has a sweet tooth when it comes to women."

Amanda placed her hands on her hips. "You're a fine one to talk. For the past year I've seen women waltz in and out of this office like it was a candy store. A little bit of this, a little bit of that," Amanda said, moving her hands in a picking motion. "Buddy, you have one hell of a sweet tooth yourself."

"I give them what they want," Mark retorted, shifting in his seat. "God, this spell has ruined everything. You used to be so reasonable, so logical, so..."

Amanda raised an eyebrow. "Manageable?"

Mark stared in stony silence. "It bothers me when he wines and dines one of my friends."

"Thank you for that small amount of insight as to why you're acting so irrationally," Amanda said, her voice calm.

A small vein pulsed on the side of his head. "I have never acted irrationally in my entire life. And for your information, the women I go out with know the score beforehand and are happy with what I give them."

"That's right!" Amanda was livid that Mark placed his wants above those of the women he dated. She no longer envied the time they spent with Mark. "They know what you want."

"What's that supposed to mean?"

"It means that when you go out, you set the rules to protect yourself. The message you give is, 'this is what I want and if you're looking for something more, then shove off'." Amanda rested her hands on his desk and leaned forward. "You don't give the women a choice. Now you're trying to impose your choice over mine."

Mark rubbed his face. "How the hell did we get so far off topic? We were discussing what you wanted."

"You haven't got a clue what I want." She was outraged that Mark could be so thoughtless.

"I can't believe that you could be interested in Tony, when only Saturday—"

Amanda straightened to her full height. "Don't even go there." She took deep breaths to compose herself. She had to stay calm or she would say something she would regret later.

With a cold, precise tone, she said, "Who said anything about feelings for Tony? I'm going out on a date with a friend. You know about friends, don't you Mark? They get together for drinks or dinner and pass the time in each other's company. You said you wanted to be my friend, so act like one."

Mark threw his pen onto his desk. "You're new to the dating game. You don't know what you want."

"And I suppose you do?" She folded her arms over her heaving chest. He was way out of line. "Friends only. Remember?"

His eyebrows disappeared into his hairline. "Fine."

"Fine." She marched to her desk and began working in icy silence.

When Tony came to pick her up before quitting time, Amanda wanted to crow when Mark's eyes widened. "You're early."

Tony chuckled. "Why so surprised?" In a white Polo shirt open at the collar, khaki pants and imported leather shoes, he looked relaxed and successful. "A very smart lady once told me that I was married to my business. That the only thing I'd be bringing to my cold bed when I got old was a healthy bank account and a shriveled heart."

Amanda's eyes widened. "Wow. That almost sounds like something my sister would say."

Tony shook his head and laughed. It sounded to Amanda as though he was laughing at himself.

"We're off," announced Tony.

"Mmm." Mark rapidly tapped his pencil against his desk.

"I'm taking Amanda to Dimmi's on Cumberland," Tony said.

"Enjoy yourselves," Mark said, returning to his work.

Tony offered Amanda his arm. "*Signorina?*"

She slipped her arm through his. "Night Mark," Amanda called over her shoulder. For her trouble she received a terse nod. Head held high, she plastered a smile on her face and strolled out of the office.

As soon as they entered the corridor, Amanda's smile dimmed.

"Chin up," Tony said, giving her hand a gentle squeeze. "The poor sucker is hooked."

"You've got it all wrong." Her throat ached with defeat.

"No, I don't. To succeed in business, I've learned to read people very well. I've never seen my friend so bewildered or agitated. Mark doesn't know it yet, but his days are numbered."

"If they are, it's not because of me."

Tony chuckled. "The way he was choking that pencil, it looked like it was about to snap in two."

Amanda heard the distinct sound of a double clang hitting the bottom of Mark's trash can.

Chapter Twelve

** හ**

"I can do this." Nervous energy zinged through Amanda as she braced herself for the awkwardness of walking into the office Wednesday morning.

Her nerves were scraped raw due to her seesawing emotions. Tightening her grip around her purse strap, she smiled at the receptionists and stepped into the office. "Good m—" she started, then froze. Empty.

She exhaled a breath she hadn't known she was holding as the oomph she'd used to psych herself with got up and left. Relief warred with disappointed that Mark wasn't there. The morning hadn't started and already she was a basket case.

On automatic pilot, Amanda turned on her computer and retrieved her phone messages. She found one from Mark telling her that he was meeting with the surveyors at the Lakeshore site and would call later in the day. Another was from Mrs. Bassett, asking if she'd get in touch with her.

Since she was alone, the first call she made was to the recruiter she had left a message with. She found out that the headhunter had already presented her qualifications to a company that wanted to hire her. Meeting with her on Friday afternoon would only be a technicality, otherwise the job was hers.

Amanda hung up and slumped in her seat. "Well, that's that." Apprehension and sadness churned within her quivering body. Her mind told her she was making the right choice while her heart slowly withered beneath her breast. But she would no longer exist on empty hopes.

Next, Amanda dialed Mrs. Bassett. "Donna? Amanda here."

"Amanda, good morning. I'll get right to the point. Mr. Bassett and I have been invited to a small sailing regatta. If you'd like, the cottage is all yours for the weekend. It's my way of making amends."

"That sounds lovely."

"Come on your own or bring a friend. The kitchen is stocked and the keys are behind the lamp next to the door."

"I'll be coming on my own, if you don't mind."

"Not at all. Treat it as though it were your own home. Once the regatta is over, Phil and I will join you for breakfast and a day together. I'll email you the directions. Bye for now," Donna said, hanging up.

Bring a friend? No chance of that happening. She pulled her chair closer to her desk and plowed through a backlog of work, determined that when she left, everything would be up-to-date. Going to the cottage would give her a chance to lick her wounds in private and strengthen her resolve to move on.

Around ten, Amanda rushed down to the main floor to grab an amaretto-flavored coffee and a bagel with chocolate cream cheese. On her way back, a shop window caught her attention. She stared at the mannequin wearing a cream-colored peignoir set that flowed to the ground. The lightness of the fabric was so transparent that a breeze could kiss it away.

What had her aunt said? It was a pity she didn't take more chances? She could see herself wearing something like that while she was at the cottage.

"Why not?" On impulse, she dashed into the store and fifteen minutes later, had a bag tucked under her arm.

On high-octane, she multitasked throughout the morning and afternoon. When the phone rang, she answered it while recalculating figures that wouldn't balance.

"Hi Amanda, how are things?"

"Hi Tony," Amanda said, distracted, assessing and comparing the columns.

"Who?" Mark's deep voice asked.

"Mark?"

"Yes." He sounded irritated.

"Sorry, I wasn't paying attention. I'm in the middle of some totals that won't add up."

Mark's voice softened. "I called to see how things were going. It's half-past two, I should be there by three at the latest."

"Is that the time? No wonder I'm hungry," Amanda said.

He checked his watch. "On the nose." Mark heard the squeak of her chair, followed by a moan and knew she was stretching. It wasn't difficult for him to visualize her body elongating as she twisted from side to side, lengthening her spine.

"Damn, I'm stiff," Amanda sighed into the phone as her chair squeaked. Mark imagined she must be settling her weight back onto it.

Stiff? "You have no idea." Ahead, the taillights of the car in front of him lit up. Mark slammed on his brakes and barely missed hitting the car.

"What did you say? I didn't quite catch that."

"I said you need to eat more," Mark said.

"I might grab another coffee."

"That's all you've had the whole day?" No wonder she was losing so much weight.

"And a bagel. I have a craving for souvlaki in a pita but that will just have to wait," Amanda said.

"See you soon." Mark clicked off.

A half-hour later, he strolled through the door waving a white bag that emitted the aroma of barbecued meat with tsaziki sauce.

"Takeout." He placed the bag on top of his desk. "It's a small peace offering."

Amanda followed. "Is that what I think it is?"

"Yes. I was hungry and thought souvlaki sounded good."

"So you skipped lunch too?" Amanda asked, taking a seat in front of Mark's desk.

"No, I didn't say that," Mark replied, passing her a pita and sitting down. "You hadn't eaten and Greek sounded like a good idea."

Mark unwrapped his souvlaki. "By the way, I just wanted you to know I heard through the company grapevine that they're down to three people for the position of Managing Director of Development. In my opinion, you're a shoo-in."

Amanda gave a small nod. "Thank you."

That's it? Mark rubbed his chin and watched as she bit into her food.

"This is amazing," she said, licking the sauce off her fingers.

He couldn't figure Amanda out. She showed more enthusiasm for her food than the tidbit he'd just dropped into her lap. Anyone else would be beside themselves. Their faces would be glowing with excitement. They'd be in a hurry to pick up the phone and share the good news. But not Amanda.

Mark brought his pita to his mouth and forgot to bite. Instead, he watched the way Amanda licked the sauce off each fingertip. Fascinated by her sensual display, Mark tried to swallow past the lump in his throat.

Her small tongue darted out to capture the sauce on her lips. With relaxed pleasure, Amanda leisurely licked the tips of her fingers again and sighed. "This is really good."

He'd never noticed before how she could turn the simple experience of eating into an erotic occurrence. Mark followed each sensual movement Amanda made, totally oblivious to the sauce dripping onto the foil wrap on his desk.

Mark shifted in his seat to ease his discomfort. Then started when Amanda took her last bite, closed her eyes and moaned.

"That hit the spot," she said, sitting back. With a swipe of her napkin, Amanda collected her garbage and tossed it into the wastebasket with a satisfied sigh.

He wanted to jump over his desk and taste Amanda.

"What?" Amanda wiped at her face. "Do I have sauce on my chin?"

"No, you're fine." *More than fine.* He sat up in his seat and with a grimace, dropped his uneaten pita back into its foil wrapper. The food in front of him was unappetizing compared to Amanda.

"You haven't touched your food."

"I guess I wasn't hungry," Mark said, shifting in his chair.

"Before I forget, Friday afternoon I have my annual doctor's checkup, so I'll be leaving during the day and coming back in the late afternoon."

Why had her cheeks pinked? "That's fine," Mark said, wrapping his food back up and throwing it away.

"Thanks for the treat. I'll finish what I was doing and then I'm out of here." Amanda stood up to leave. "I have things to do tonight."

"Anything special?" Mark leaned back in his chair and pretended an indifference he didn't feel. He'd just wait for the spell to kick in and the truth would come out of her mouth.

"Not really. I'm driving Aunt Lilly around to get some things for her trip."

Bingo. Mark smirked. "Your aunt and Emily are still going? How did they accomplish that?"

Amanda shrugged. "Plain stubbornness. Aunt Lilly is trying to convince Sarah to go along."

Mark chuckled. "Your aunt never ceases to amaze me."

"I think it's kinda cute. If Sarah meets up with someone on the ship, Aunt Lilly and Emily can act as chaperones."

"You mean the other way around," Mark said, shaking his head. "I have a feeling that Sarah's hands will be full keeping those dears out of trouble."

"You're a pessimist. You'll see," Amanda predicted.

"It will be interesting, to say the least," Mark commented, watching Amanda return to her desk.

"Interesting," she said. A bright grin painted her face as she peered at her computer.

"What is?"

"I just completed steps three and five from a list my aunt made."

What list? She wasn't making sense. He shook his head and got back to work. Maybe the magic affected more than just her mouth.

That evening, Tony stuck his head through the door. "You have any plans for tonight?" he asked Amanda.

"She's busy with her aunt," Mark snapped. "And shouldn't you be at work like the rest of us?"

Tony just grinned at him. "The whole night?"

"I'll be finished by eight. What do you have in mind?" Amanda asked.

"Remember how I told you at the picnic that I had a weakness for ice cream?"

She nodded.

"There's a new dessert place that lets you create your own masterpieces that I thought we could try."

"Count me in."

"I'll pick you up at your house. Later," Tony waved at Mark and disappeared.

"See you tomorrow." Grabbing her purse, Amanda left for the day.

Mark threw his pen onto his desk. "The bastard did it again." A war of emotions raged within him. After Amanda accepted her promotion, he was taking her out for that long overdue celebration.

Friday afternoon, Mark got caught in a downpour as he paid for his taxi and ran for the revolving doors of his office building. The smell of silk and starch from his drenched clothes hit his nose and rain dripped off his hair onto his face as he entered the elevator. "Come on, come on." He willed the increasing floor numbers to hurry up.

As soon as the doors edged open, Mark rushed off the elevator and grimaced at the feel of his saturated socks in his expensive, Italian leather shoes. "Ladies," he nodded to Misty and Cindy, and kept moving.

Today was the big day. His erratic heartbeat picked up speed. Today, Amanda would get her promotion and together they could celebrate. He dropped his briefcase on Amanda's desk and with a snap, opened it and took out a gold-wrapped gift, centering it on her desk so that it would be the first thing she saw when she returned from her doctor's appointment.

It was a gold bracelet with a charm shaped like a magic wand. The minute he'd seen it, he'd thought of Amanda and bought it. He no longer begrudged the spell Amanda's aunt had cast. Instead, he'd come to appreciate Amanda's hidden talents and was looking forward to discovering what other treasures she had concealed.

Excitement kissed his skin with goose bumps and sent his heart racing. Turning toward his office, he tripped over a bag on the side of Amanda's desk and sent the contents sliding out.

Picking the garment off the floor, shock hit him full force as he stared at the transparent nightgown. "What the hell?"

He held it with the tips of his fingers and growled. From the look of things Amanda had already implemented his suggestion to find the man of her dreams. What he'd like to know was who? The only man he'd seen her go out with was his best— "Son of a bitch." Mark shoved the nightgown back into the bag.

"Who're you cussing?" Tony leaned in the doorway, his eyes alight with devilish merriment. "And is it safe to come in?"

"I'm cussing no one in particular. I just have a lot of things on my mind." Denial flew through Mark. Not his friend. He should just come out and ask him.

"'Things' as in a person?" Tony asked.

"I have no idea what you're talking about."

Tony shrugged. "Have it your way."

Mark clenched his fists at his sides. The temptation to slug Tony's pretty face was overwhelming. "Are you sleeping with Amanda?" he blurted.

Tony threw his head back and laughed. "No I'm not." He shook his head and chuckled. "Boy, you have it bad. Whatever gave you that idea?"

Mark picked up the bag and dropped it on top of Amanda's desk, waving Tony closer.

Tony looked inside and whistled.

Mark pulled his fingers through his hair. "Tell me about it."

"Damn, she's got good taste." Tony lifted the lingerie out of the bag for a closer look.

"Give me that." Mark snatched it out of his hands and stuffed it back into the bag. "If you're not sleeping with her and I'm not, then who is?"

"Maybe it's someone here."

"Nah." Forget it. That would mean that the romance had been going on under his nose and he'd been too blind and stupid to notice it.

As if on cue, Greg came charging into the room, red-faced and waving a paper in front of him. "Did you guys see this? I'd like to get my hands on whoever did it."

"May I?" Tony asked, taking the still-flapping paper out of Greg's hands and reading it. "Insensitive, six-foot two-inch, blond, brown-eyed office gigolo wishes to reform. For constructive criticism send all remarks to—" It ended with Greg's email address. Chuckling, Tony passed the paper to Mark.

"I don't see what's so funny. This message has been emailed to everyone in this office building," Greg said.

"How many women have you offended enough that they'd want to get even with you?" Tony asked.

Turning a deeper shade of red, Greg looked away. "I don't know what you're talking about."

Tony glanced at him. "Another one with a memory chip missing."

"Let's face it Greg, you don't have the best reputation when it comes to treating women right," Mark said.

Greg backpedaled. "It still doesn't give whoever wrote this garbage the right to email it on my behalf."

"How hard would it be to narrow it down?" Tony asked.

"How many emails have you received so far?" Mark asked.

"Close to fifty. Forty women—some answering twice—and ten men. Five of them telling me it's guys like me who give the good guys a bad rap and the other five wanted me to get in touch with my feminine side."

Tony opened his mouth to say something but Mark shook his head to shut him up. With a shrug, Tony leaned against Amanda's desk and crossed his ankles, making himself comfortable.

"Let's do some process of elimination. Ten were from men, so that brings it down to forty. How many were duplicates?" Mark asked.

"Twelve of them," Greg said.

"So you're down to twenty-eight annoyed women," concluded Mark.

Tony whistled. "Not bad."

"Shut up." Greg's face burned red. "I think Amanda did this. I know she doesn't like me."

Mark narrowed his eyes and in a menacing voice asked, "And why would that be? Is there something you've done that I should know about?"

"I've never laid a finger on her."

"Amanda wouldn't do such a thing," Tony said, straightening away from the desk and taking a step toward Greg. "She's the type of person who would prefer to tell you to your face what she doesn't like, rather than stab you in the back. *Capisci?*"

"Besides, I would know about it," Mark said, thinking of the spell. Mark handed the piece of paper back to Greg. "Next time you decide to step over the boundaries, think again. Because if I find out about it, you'll be sorry."

Greg stormed out of the office, the rapid whispers of the receptionists following him. Mark rubbed his throbbing temple. Didn't anyone have work to do? "Ladies?" Their heads snapped toward him. "Is there something that I should know about?"

"No." Two heads shook in denial. He didn't trust their angelic smiles.

Mark gave a tired sigh. "Never mind." He walked to his bathroom, turned on the faucet and popped two aspirins into his mouth.

Tony followed. "I should drop in more often. Your life is quite entertaining."

"My life is normally dull, so don't make a habit of showing up unannounced. Besides, shouldn't you be at work instead of spending so much time at my office, sniffing around Amanda?"

"Girlfriend," Tony said, affecting a high-pitched, urban female accent, "you are in trouble with a capital T." He gave Mark's shoulder a friendly slap. "Can I give you some advice without getting my head bit off?"

"No. But I'm sure you're going to tell me anyway."

"She's a keeper," Tony said, following Mark into his office. "If that's what you want, then go for it. If not, back off so that some deserving chap can have a chance."

"Would you be this deserving chap?" Mark wanted to punch that grin off his friend's face. "Not on your life."

"Then don't let her get away. I made the same mistake and let Sarah slip through my fingers."

"Sarah? Amanda's sister!?" Pain flickered in his best friend's eyes. Damn, he thought he knew his friend so well. It seemed that Anthony had held this information close to his chest. "How come you've never mentioned her before?"

Anthony shook his head. "She was too important to share." He slapped Mark on the back. "Let me know how things turn out," Tony said, walking out of his office.

The smile on Mark's face grew to a wolfish grin. "Amanda's not going anywhere." He strolled into Amanda's office and slipped the gift into his pocket. He'd give it to her over dinner. Reaching into the lingerie bag again, Mark took one last peek.

Amanda huddled under her umbrella and rushed toward her office building. Pedestrians hastened into doorways and waiting taxis to get out of the rain. She stepped into a puddle with her open, high-heeled sandals and felt the water swish in between her toes.

The gray skies lit with a flash of lightning, followed by an ominous rumble. The thunderstorm matched her mood. Not an hour ago she'd accepted a new job. She should be ecstatic, but she wasn't. Instead, she was confused with the speed that things had changed and angry that nothing had worked out like she had hoped.

Enclosing herself in a wall of determination, Amanda straightened her shoulders and entered the lobby of her building. This was for the best. A new job, a new life, a new man. Now that Amanda knew she could accomplish anything, nothing and no one could stand in her way.

Amanda closed her umbrella and held it away from her, letting it drip on the granite floor as she walked onto the elevator. Stepping off on her floor, she shook the umbrella one last time and hurried to her office. "I'm back—" She came to an abrupt stop.

Holding up her cream-colored peignoir set was Mark. His flushed face contrasted with the soft color of the garment in front of him.

"The color doesn't do a thing for you," Amanda said, marching into the office.

"What?" The thunder in Mark's voice made the receptionists jump in their seats. Cindy and Misty stared at him still holding up the negligee.

Mark stuffed the offending garment back into the bag and thrust it toward Amanda. "You have impeccable taste."

She placed the bag on her desk, vowing this time that she wouldn't forget to take it home. "Have you lost your mind? What were you doing looking through my things?"

If it was possible, his face burned a deeper red. "I tripped over it by accident. When I lifted it off the floor, the contents fell out."

Amanda tried to sidestep Mark, but he purposely blocked her way. "Do you mind?" she asked, aiming a glacial look at him. "I'd like to get to my seat."

"No."

That one quiet word sounded like a shotgun. Amanda jerked in shock and took a step back.

Mark advanced and gently took hold of her arms, holding her in front of him. The silence thrummed against her nerves. "I don't have time for this nonsense."

"That's fine by me, you don't have to talk, just listen."

Amanda's eyes narrowed to slits. "Excuse me?"

"Please. I'm trying to apologize for my behavior. All I can say in my defense is that lately I haven't been thinking straight."

"You haven't been thinking at all," Amanda said, pulling out of his grasp.

"Follow me." Mark took a step back so she could walk into his office.

Amanda could see that he was back to boss mode. She sat in front of his desk and clasped her hands together.

Mark settled behind his desk and cleared his throat. "The reason I asked you into my office is to give you some good news." His voice filled with excitement as his smile grew into a grin.

Amanda's knuckles turned white. She already knew what was coming.

Twirling his pen between his fingers, Mark confidently delivered his announcement. "Amanda, you got the promotion."

When she didn't return his grin, it turned into a frown. "Amanda? You did it. Once you're installed in your new office, we can finally go for that drink you asked about. What do you say to that?"

"I'm handing in my two-week notice of resignation."

"What?" he blurted, his mouth hanging open.

"I said —"

"I heard what you said. What I want to know is why?"

"Because I have accepted another job." Amanda relished each syllable that slipped from her lips, tasting triumph when the pen slipped out of Mark's hands. She hardened her heart when he slumped in his seat and stared at her like she had lost her head.

She finally had his full, undivided attention.

Chapter Thirteen

ઐ

The world was going mad.

Mark jabbed Amanda's doorbell several times, then resumed his frantic pacing. He fisted his hands in his pants pockets so he wouldn't surrender to the urge to hit a wall.

Absolute, stark raving madness, that's what this was. He couldn't reason away the existence of a spell, nor could he understand Amanda's bizarre behavior when she'd dropped her bomb. "Resign?" He threw his hands out and let them drop to his sides. "Ridiculous."

No one in their right mind would throw away a brilliant career. Obviously, Amanda could and did. And like a fool, he'd stared, thunderstruck, in numb acceptance. No other woman had ever left him speechless.

Mark pressed down on the doorbell and kept his finger there. "Come on, come on."

He'd been an idiot. By the time he'd emerged from his stunned confusion Amanda had left. A tumble of bewildering thoughts and feelings had raced through him. Fear had led the race as waves of panic had washed over his mind and sent his heart floundering into the deep end.

He'd tried to get rid of the spell and rearrange her life to his liking and instead had pushed her too far. Life had kicked him in the butt when Amanda had burned rubber out of his office, leaving him with a mouthful of grit.

He banged on the door. "Anybody home?" he yelled. If no one answered he didn't know where else to look. He didn't even know Amanda's cell phone number.

"Hold your horses."

Through the opaque stained glass window, Mark could distinguish Aunt Lilly's robust body toddling toward him. "Thank God," he murmured as relief poured over his frazzled nerves. He could finally straighten out this mess.

The door burst open, presenting a gold-turbaned Aunt Lilly holding the ends of her candle-filled apron in one hand, while wielding a barbecue lighter in the other. "You." She poked him in the chest with the lighter. "You went and blew it, buster. Big time."

Mark pushed the lighter aside before she decided to set him on fire. "I need to speak to Amanda."

"Forget it." Aunt Lilly tapped her slippered foot. "Besides, she's not here."

He peered past her, hoping to see any telltale movement down the hallway. "Where is she?" He didn't believe this sly, little old woman one bit. Not after knowing the trouble she could cause.

"I haven't got a clue," Lilly said, picking flower petals and melted wax off her apron. "Now, if you don't mind, I'm in the middle of something."

From the looks of things Lilly was up to her old tricks again. With her turban and candles it looked like he had caught her in the middle of casting another spell. "Perhaps Sarah would know." Mark wasn't leaving until he got his answer.

Aunt Lilly nervously scanned the area over his shoulder. "I sent her on a whole bunch of errands, so she'll be awhile. A long while. So, good-bye."

He stopped the door from closing with his foot, then pushed it open again. *The little liar. Two could play this game.* "Here's the deal. If you tell me where Amanda is, I promise not to tell Sarah that I found you up to your hocus-pocus tricks again."

Her round double chin jutted out in an obstinate challenge. "I'll deny it. Besides, why should I tell you anything? You made it perfectly clear that you didn't want Amanda. So bugger off."

Mark held the door while Lilly used her weight as leverage to close it on him. "Please, I need to talk to her." His desperation must have come across, for Lilly stopped pushing and let the door slowly reopen. A pair of cynical eyes scrutinized him.

"She's gone." Sadness passed over Lilly's features. "She packed an overnight bag and hightailed out of here."

Guilt settled in the pit of his stomach, overwhelming him, tightening each nerve ending. "I really need to find her." He had done this to her, forced her to find solace elsewhere.

"You planning on hurting her again?"

"I've never intentionally set out to hurt her."

"Intentionally?" Aunt Lilly snorted. "You can keep your noble plans if this is how they work out. Hell, your tactics fail worse than mine do and that's saying something."

Didn't he know it. "I have to make this right with her," he pleaded.

He wanted to move forward with Amanda, but nothing too serious. Right? He didn't want to move too quickly and have the same scenario with Amanda that he'd had with his previous girlfriends.

Aunt Lilly gave a resigned sigh. "All I know is that she went to some cottage built for a bunch of hound dogs," she grumbled. "Some people have more money than sense, building a cottage for their pets."

Mark rubbed his hands over his face. "Hound dogs? Aunt Lilly, do you mean the Bassetts?" *Did this woman ever get anything straight?*

"That's them."

"Thank you!" Mark exclaimed, hugging her off her feet and giving her a quick kiss on the cheek.

"Put me down."

"I owe you one," he said and ran to his car. He'd been to the Bassetts' cottage a couple of times. With any luck he'd be able to get there before nightfall.

Amanda navigated her car down a low riverbank, over smooth rocks covered by a calm trickle of water, then pressed the gas and climbed the opposite incline. She followed along the dirt road flanked by a dense, towering forest.

She rounded a bend and the cottage appeared beneath the late afternoon sun. "Wow. This is a cottage?" It looked more like a luxury home to her.

Turning off the engine, she just sat there and stared. The cottage had a southern design, with a welcoming front porch, rustic brick façade and a shingled roof with five dormer windows. Four large bay windows flanked a bright red front door with a brass knocker.

This place was perfect for her to begin to heal. Amanda grabbed her overnight case from the front seat and stepped out of the car.

She inhaled the sweet fragrance of wildflowers. The surrounding trees were filled with the sounds of nature. She needed this.

Since she had walked out of the office and away from Mark's accepting silence, her body and heart had been locked in misery. Her shoulders were knotted with suppressed tension. Not even the long ride into the country had helped soothe her.

She couldn't get over Mark's unresponsive attitude. He hadn't even opened his mouth to persuade her to stay. His insensitivity had cemented her decision.

Amanda easily found the key and walked into a gigantic, two-story, sun-filled room. "Amazing," she said, dropping her case by the stairs.

The lingering smell of cinnamon teased her senses as her eyes came across a blanket on the floor next to an overflowing toy box. Groupings of family pictures were everywhere. She instinctively knew that the house and its occupants were cherished and well loved.

She strolled into an open-concept room, the front of it filled with a large arrangement of sofas and chairs, along with a pool table and foosball table. The kitchen sat at the back of the room, where a table and chairs sat in front of a sliding-glass door leading to a deck and the lake.

Amanda picked up a cue and imitated the position of pool players on TV. "Six ball in the corner pocket." She aimed and missed. Carefully, Amanda put the cue back down. "And maybe not."

Running her fingers over a large-screen TV, she admired the floor-to-ceiling bookshelves crammed tight with well-read books beside a fieldstone fireplace. Sofas and chairs were positioned so that people could either join in the fun of playing pool, or relax and watch.

A deep yearning overwhelmed her. This room, this cottage, was built with family in mind. She thought of Mark, but longing for what she would never have with him was useless. Amanda pushed on.

Opening a door off the left side of the kitchen, she spotted the laundry room. Back toward the front of the house, another door led to a master suite and Donna's studio.

Entering the studio, Amanda smelled the faint odor of oil paints and turpentine. Easels were lined up against the walls, each picture a fragile memory captured on a thin layer of cloth. Around and around Amanda turned, surrounded by someone else's life's instances.

One painting depicted the cottage lake in the early morning hours, with a light, ghostly mist still settled on the surface of the water. Others showed children playing. Another showed large terra-cotta pots overflowing with wildflowers. She instantly realized that Donna was one very talented lady.

Amanda bent down and caressed the lines of a particular oil painting. It depicted a golden-haired little girl kneeling beside a tree stump, trying to encourage a turtle out of its shell. "Beautiful."

These paintings were someone else's past. Amanda stood up. "It's time I make my future." Determined to make her own memories, Amanda headed for the stairs. It was easy to admire talent, but futile to covet another person's life. She was here to create her own.

Upstairs, Amanda found two guest bedrooms with an adjoining bathroom. She chose the one simply decorated with a queen poster bed and a dresser. A rich, Oriental rug in hues of gold complemented the blue of the walls and the honey-toned wooden floors.

She dropped her luggage onto the bed and headed to the washroom. It was wall-to-wall granite. An enormous shower that could easily accommodate two adults stood in the corner. Beneath a bay window stood the biggest sunken bathtub she had ever seen. It even had a telephone and stereo system at arm's length. Go figure.

"What's this?" A gift basket sat on the counter, next to the sink. Picking up the card, she read, *Amanda, for your enjoyment.*

It was filled with scented candles, chocolates, bubble bath, two glasses with a bottle of wine, and a tube of body paint.

"I'll make sure it doesn't go to waste." Amanda broke the cellophane and opened a box of truffles.

She popped one into her mouth, letting the rich European chocolate coat her tongue. A decadent wave of creamy bliss slid down her throat as she returned to her bedroom.

"Oh, these are so deadly." She chose a truffle filled with creamy coffee liqueur and popped it into her mouth, heading to a window to see the view.

She found a crystal clear lake that reflected the boulders and trees along its shore. A long wooden dock reached out into the water, boasting two inviting Muskoka chairs.

Filled with restless excitement, Amanda quickly changed into her bathing suit, found a large, fluffy towel, remembered the box of truffles and hurried back downstairs. Before heading out, she grabbed a wine cooler from the large sub-zero fridge in the kitchen.

Walking through the sliding doors, Amanda looked over the tranquil lake. The water sparkled like diamonds. A fish jumped into the air and made a small splash, leaving in its wake expanding circles on the surface. Strolling down the dock, she inhaled the rich fragrance of pine and damp earth.

Getting comfortable on one of the chairs, Amanda ate another truffle and saluted the lake with her bottle. "To me."

A gentle breeze teased her soft curls in front of her face. In the distance, a motorboat sped through the water, its sound echoing in the tranquility. The surface foamed with expanding waves, making the water splash against the dock, gently rocking it.

Inhaling deeply, Amanda relaxed further into her chair. "This is the life." The day's tension finally dissipated, filling her with a quiet resolve.

Twisting the cap off the bottle, she took a sip. It was full-steam ahead from here. If she was honest with herself, because of the spell, she would have had to leave eventually. Mark knew about her feelings for him and even if he didn't want to hurt her, she would have ended up another woman in his line of conquests.

And that was something she wouldn't have let happen. The spell had only sped up the process. It had forced her to stand up for herself, inevitably building up her courage and self-esteem.

Since she was leaving in two weeks, the least she could have done was have an affair with Mark and get him out of her system. That's the usual length of time some of his women lasted. But she couldn't handle that. And it really burned her that Mark was finally willing to mix business with pleasure because of the promotion. It hadn't been convenient for Mark before and it sure as hell wasn't acceptable to her now.

Dropping the truffles and bottle onto the deck, Amanda stood and made a running leap off the edge of the dock. "Geronimo!" she yelled, and cannon-balled into the water. She came up laughing. On impulse, she squirmed out of her bathing suit and threw it onto the dock. "Ha, now *this* is spontaneous."

This was what life was all about. Living with yourself and your decisions. Accepting the challenges and running with them.

"Hello, world," Amanda shouted, "look at me now."

Swimming leisurely, Amanda enjoyed the new sensation of water lapping against her sensitive skin. Like a lover's hands, the soft, flowing movement of the water made her tingle. After half an hour, she felt a peace embrace her that reflected the surroundings.

Getting tired, Amanda checked to see if anyone was around before climbing the ladder on the side of the dock and hauling herself out of the water. "Brrr." A breeze covered her in goose bumps as water trickled down her body to puddle on the dock where she stood drying herself with her towel.

Relaxed, Amanda gathered her things and strolled to the cottage, letting the breeze stroke her skin. She hung her towel and bathing suit over the deck railing to dry.

It was exhilarating walking around *au naturel*. "Ha, who said I don't have any confidence?" Amanda popped another truffle in her mouth and opened the sliding door to the cottage. Leaving her empty bottle on the table, she was opening the fridge for another cooler when she heard the sound of a car door slamming.

Her ears pricked up, listening for any other sound. Cautiously placing her bottle and chocolates on the table, she inched sideways until she could see out one of the front windows — and saw Mark jogging up the front steps.

"Oh shit!"

She wouldn't make it in time to lock the front door. On slippery feet, she slid to the laundry room and jumped through the door, slamming it shut as the front door burst open.

"Amanda?"

"Yes?" She covered her overactive mouth to muffle her voice. "Shut up, shut up." She wished she could find something to stuff down her throat.

Frantically, she looked around the laundry room. The clean, spotless, no-dirty-clothes laundry room. What normal person didn't have dirty clothes?

Stepping away from the door, she opened the dryer then the washing machine to see if there were clothes within. Nothing. Recklessly, she opened closets and drawers. "Come on, come on. If there ever was a time I needed a miracle, it's now."

She was running out of options and time. Chemicals, cleaners, fishing boots, rods and reels. But no clothes.

"Amanda?"

She groaned. "That's my name," she whispered. Desperate, she leaned against the door and prayed that Mark would go outside to search for her so that she could make a mad dash for the stairs.

"Where the hell are you?"

She covered her face. "In the laundry room with my big, fat mouth." So much for the power of prayer. She was her own worst enemy. If she ever joined the army, she could work for the enemy and give their position away.

Amanda watched the handle turn and pressed her full weight against the door. "Go away."

Mark let go of the door handle. The apprehension in her voice clawed at his body. "Amanda, quit hiding and come out. We need to talk about what happened this afternoon. You can't just resign from your job."

"You bet I can. I didn't walk away from my job—I'm running toward my future."

"This is ridiculous." He refused to talk to a door. "Damn it Amanda, why won't you open this door?" Mark asked, rattling the knob.

"Because I'm naked, you jackass."

His hand jerked from the knob as he stepped back. "Holy crap." An image of Amanda behind the door blasted through his mind and detonated the fuse in his body. It was then that he spotted the two bottles on the kitchen table. "Are you alone?"

The notion of another man being here with Amanda overwhelmed him with possessiveness. The very thought of *any* man trying to get to first base with Amanda made Mark's hands fist. Since she'd only recently come out of her shell, Amanda needed protecting. And he would be the one to help in that department.

"Yes," Amanda snapped. "What kind of stupid question is that?"

"Because I see two bottles, that's why."

"Oh."

That's all? Oh? Mark pulled his fingers through his hair. "Why are you naked?"

He heard a tired sigh from the other side of the door. "I went skinny-dipping and when I came in, you showed up."

Mark paced in front of the door. "Isn't there anything in there you could throw on?"

"No, Einstein, there isn't. Don't you think I would have put it on by now if there was? Or do you think I get my kicks freezing my ass off while you yell at me."

"For crying out loud," Mark said, pulling his black silk shirt out of his pants and unbuttoned it. "Use this."

The door inched open just enough so that he could stick his hand through. As soon as Amanda snatched the shirt, Mark pulled his hand back before he lost his fingers.

He leaned against the back of a sofa and warily rubbed his face. "What a mess." His head snapped up at the sound of the door opening.

Amanda stood there looking at him wearily with her arms defensively wrapped around her waist. The silk of the shirt clung to her body and barely covered her thighs. Her dark, wet hair cascaded down her back.

"How did you know where to find me?" she asked, her pale beauty frozen into alert stillness.

"Your aunt told me." She was stunning. When had the sweet, quiet Amanda and the candidly beautiful Amanda merged into one?

This is what he'd lost—not Amanda the assistant, but this woman. He'd let his hang-ups get in the way and let this vulnerable creature standing in front of him slip through his fingers. "Why don't you go take a hot shower, then we'll talk. How does that sound?"

"It sucks." She skirted around him and walked backward toward the stairs, holding his shirt down. Her actions only made the shirt became a second skin.

"By the time I come down, I want you gone."

"You can't say that and just walk away," he said, taking a few steps toward her.

"Watch me."

"Watch you?" Mark's breath hissed through his clenched teeth. Eating up the distance, he pulled her into his arms. "That's all I've done."

Amanda pushed against his chest. "Oh, you've done more than that."

"I've been patient and understanding while you've acted totally out of character because of this damn spell." Mark held her firmly in place. "And so that I wouldn't confuse you, I've given you space."

"Give me a break," she sneered, her lips twisting into a cynical smile. "You kept your distance because you weren't sure what would come out of my mouth. When I asked you to kiss me, you ran in the opposite direction."

"You were moving too fast," he explained, smoothing his hands up and down her arms. "Besides, I'm here now."

"Forget it."

He felt the heat travel up his neck and settle on his cheeks. "Forget it?" Had he heard her right? "You're kidding right?"

"No." Her answer was plain and simple for a situation that was anything but.

"Earlier it was yes, now it's no?"

"That's correct. I see there's nothing wrong with your hearing."

Anger, desire and the need to change her mind exploded into one. With a guttural sound, Mark captured her mouth with all his pent-up passion and tasted chocolate.

Amanda snapped her head back. "You should have done this when you had the chance."

Mark clasped the back of her neck and brought his lips next to hers. "Maybe my brain finally caught up with the rest of me."

"Well my mind doesn't want this." Angry tremors shook her.

"And your body?" he asked, kissing the side of her neck and blowing in her ear. "Does it want this?"

"No," she said in a tortured whisper.

He swirled a curl behind her ear and inhaled Amanda's mysterious scent. He lifted her chin and placed gentle kisses across her face. "This?" He nipped Amanda's earlobe. A telling gasp filled her chest.

Her nails dug into his arms. "Unfortunately."

Amanda pulled him close. Encouraged by her boldness, Mark traced the shape of her ear with his tongue. Her soft whimper echoed around them as she melted in his arms. His breathing quickened to match Amanda's as his heartbeat pulsed at the base of his neck.

Her chest rose and fell in short, rapid breaths. He had fantasized about her, but nothing had prepared him for Amanda's trusting beauty. Her features reflected every emotion.

Mark possessively moved closer. It thrilled him that she was so receptive to him. "I've dreamed about this. Any fantasies I should know about?"

"Would you happen to have any oil?" she asked, her eyes challenging him.

His heart nearly jumped out of his chest. "Did you say oil?"

Amanda gave a nod.

Through clenched teeth, Mark released his breath and groaned. "Now she tells me."

A devilish look came into her eyes. "Next time."

He began his slow assault on her senses. He gently kissed her forehead, over flushed cheeks, down to her neck. Mark could feel the flutter of her heart keeping pace with each kiss. Amanda tilted her head back and encouraged him on.

She pulled at his shoulders, trying to gain access to his lips. But he had his own agenda. He traced the shape of her face and returned to her ear. His tongue slowly licked its shell before dipping in. Amanda moaned and imitated a more erotic motion with her own body.

Wrapping her fingers through his hair, she leaned into him. He tasted sweetness. A soft whimper of frustration floated between them. Amanda's pulse beat under his tongue. He was almost at his limit.

"Open for me," he demanded, licking the seam of her swollen lips.

Amanda eagerly blossomed beneath his lips. Angling his mouth for a deeper position, Mark savored her. She was a craving he could get addicted to. One taste wasn't going to be enough for him.

He captured the weight of her breast in his hand and felt the heavy beat of her heart against his palm. It sent a message pulsating through his body. His fantasies hadn't even come close. Mark soothed his hands down her back and firmly cupped her bottom, holding her against the evidence of his hardened penis.

A moan of surrender shook Amanda as she buried her face against the corded muscles of his chest. The brush of cool silk and soft curves sent his temperature climbing. Waves of heat radiated off his body to liquefy hers.

Heart pounding, Mark swept Amanda into his arms and laid her on the sofa before stretching out beside her. Her pliant softness teased his heated chest. Her small hands stroking his senses higher. His body shook with emotions too long suppressed—denied. Hunger gnawed like an awakened animal, roaring to be fed.

Mark unbuttoned her shirt and separated its sides. Like a precious gift, he revealed Amanda's flushed body to his famished senses. "God you're beautiful."

He drew her breast into his mouth and rolled her hardened nipple, squeezing it between his lips. With a cry, Amanda clasped his head to her and arched her back off the sofa. Her open response intoxicated him. Reclaiming her lips, Mark crushed her softness to him. Her trembling limbs clung to his slightest touch. Mark could feel Amanda's uneven breathing on his chest as he held her close. His self-control unraveled as his world crumbled.

He fondled her breast again, its soft weight a treasure. Her moans drawing him closer, his tongue caressed her sensitive swollen nipples. Amanda entwined her fingers in his hair and held him there. Fire burst against his tongue as her breasts surged at the intimacy of his touch. His hands searched for pleasure points, teasing more cries from her throat.

Beads of sweat formed on his forehead, his breathing accelerated as his heartbeat soared. Everything was happening too quickly. Amanda's transformation had devastated him. Worse was his overwhelming need to keep her close to him.

Hunger drove him on. Her smell, her taste—like a thirsty man, he drank her in. He caressed and kissed each inch his eyes feasted on. The urgency to show her that she belonged with him became his primal impulse. He hadn't thought this far ahead, but going back was no longer an option.

Her skin quivered beneath his touch. He sucked in his stomach when her hand reached between them, sliding into the front of his pants and clasping him. The cool touch of her fingers sent him over the edge.

He sprang to his feet, pulled out the condom he carried in his wallet and stripped off his pants. Amanda's eyes devoured him. She reached out and ran her finger along his length, making his penis jerk with pleasure. Brushing her hand aside, Mark rolled on his condom settled between Amanda's thighs.

Slowly penetrating her tight opening, he found warm, slick dampness. Inserting only a few inches of his penis, he moved in and out of her, her inner muscles clasping his length. Sweat dripped off his face as he controlled his movements so he wouldn't hurt her.

She wrapped her legs around his waist and tightened their grip, surging up to take him in completely. Her eyes widened as his full length filled her. "Okay?" he asked, stilling his movements so she could get used to him.

"Please…" She shivered and shook beneath him. Her hands kneaded his shoulders. Her small animal sounds brought him closer to the edge. "Don't stop."

His slow rhythm changed to a frenzied pace. His groans mingled with her cries of ecstasy. His mouth ravished her swollen lips. He could feel the heat building. In his body. In hers. Where they were joined.

With a scream, Amanda convulsed around him. Her inner walls milked him. Straining, he pumped into her until a white-hot climax shot through him. He threw his head back and growled his pleasure. He supported his weight on shaking arms until his tremors subsided.

"You are amazing," he gasped, collapsing beside her and pulling her close to his side. He shifted away to dispose of the condom, then angled their bodies spoon-style, so he wouldn't crush her.

"Wow." Her body quivered against him.

As their breathing returned to normal, shivers of warmth escaped their heated skin as they cooled down. Mark closed his shirt around Amanda's body and hugged her.

Lifting his head onto his hand, Mark placed his finger under Amanda's chin and gently made her face him. "We're perfect together."

A delightful blush of satisfaction was her answer.

Mark lifted a stray curl off her forehead and smiled at her. "I think we should explore what we have and take it slow. You should take that promotion the company is offering you, so we can continue to see each other."

Amanda pushed him away and sat up. Her eyes were thunderous. "So that I can become one of your lady friends? No thanks." She buttoned her shirt with shaking fingers. "This…we…what just happened, didn't change anything. I'm still leaving."

Mark stood up and pulled on his pants. "For the love of—" He snapped his mouth shut. "What we just shared doesn't change anything?"

"No." Her quick response sliced into him. Amanda edged off the sofa and backed away. A stark paleness replaced her previously contented blush. "Oh my God, you're not the one." She held his stare, her hand fluttering against her chest.

"What do you mean I'm not the one?" Mark pulled his fingers through his hair. "You can stand there and tell me I'm not the one after what we just did?"

"Yes," Amanda replied in a tormented whisper.

"Why?" He felt for the edge of a chair and collapsed into it.

"Because I'm still answering your questions. Because if you had been the one, the spell would be broken." Longing lay naked in her eyes. "Don't you remember what the spell said? 'Once everything is said and done, then you'll find your only one'." Amanda pulled her hands through her hair. "The words are still coming out of my mouth."

"Maybe the spell needs more time to realize that it's time for it to split."

"And maybe it's time for you to leave." Unshed tears shone in her eyes as Amanda rushed up the stairs.

Mark winced. She meant it—otherwise she wouldn't have said it. Where had he gone wrong? Sweat beaded on his upper lip. He didn't know what he should do next.

How could he convince her to explore what they had and build from there? To take it slow? She'd given him so many chances, expressed her feelings in so many ways, and what had he done? Rejected her.

Her words sank in. Not the one. Fear clutched his heart and squeezed each pounding beat until he couldn't breathe. The spell was proof that he wasn't her true love, and they couldn't move forward with the damn thing still attached to Amanda.

A slow, feral smile grew on his face as an idea formed. His determination intensified.

Then he'd have to break the damn thing.

Chapter Fourteen

အာ

Mark wasn't the one.

Sadness shook Amanda's frail composure, rattling her frayed nerves. She took deep breaths to calm her anxieties. Transfixed at the top of the stairs, with her hair in a ponytail and wearing a camel-colored, floor-length knit dress, she listened to Mark banging drawers in the kitchen.

How could she have been so wrong? If he had been the one, the spell would have broken and she wouldn't have answered his questions. Lost in misery, Amanda took a tired step down.

She'd just had the best sex of her life with the wrong man. Her mind and body staggered with bewilderment. Gripping the railing, she forced her feet down each step. She didn't know what to think anymore.

Mark met her in the family room holding two margaritas. Terrible regret assailed her just looking at him. "I asked you to leave, not make yourself comfortable." He had changed into a pair of jeans and a white T-shirt, and lit candles to illuminate the kitchen in a warm soft glow.

"I'm not leaving." Mark passed her a glass and waved her to one of the sofas. With the evening growing cold, he'd lit a fire in the fireplace. The light of the flames danced across the walls and windows, creating an orange cover of warmth.

Amanda sidestepped Mark and placed her drink on the table in front of the fire, before settling onto the sofa and hugging her legs to her chest. Mark sat next to her and placed his glass next to hers.

Mark rested his elbows on his knees and rubbed his face. "Where should I start?"

"Anywhere you want."

Taking a deep breath, he did. "I think I'm a reasonably logical man. But ever since the spell, I haven't been able to think straight."

"You think you've had it bad? How do you think I've felt?"

"I know. I kept hoping that things would return to normal. Our office routine, your distracting appearance—"

"My big, fat mouth," Amanda interrupted, taking a sip from her melting margarita.

Mark had the grace to look guilty. "Especially that. But the more you changed, the more addicted I became. I found myself anticipating your arrival at work to see what you wore. I listened for the next time your candidness would get the better of you. I was hooked."

"I don't understand where this is going." Each word Mark spoke was like a nail hammered into her heart.

"I'm getting there." He sat back and rested his arm behind her, shifting his knee onto the sofa. "My problem, like Emily guessed, is that I think too much. I kept the two images of the new and old Amanda separate in my mind. When I finally overlapped the two, I realized that you were one and the same."

Well, bully for him. "I'm so glad you straightened yourself out."

"There's more. You said I didn't know what I wanted. Well, I do."

Amanda's eyes rounded. That statement got her attention like nothing else could. Heart pounding, Amanda could only stare. His eyes mirrored honesty and hesitation. Determination and vulnerability. Amanda couldn't believe that he was finally opening up to her. She tightened her numb fingers around her frosty glass.

"When you said I set the rules so that I could hide behind them, you were right. As soon as a woman wanted more, I backed out of the relationship. I did the same thing with you."

Amanda looked away. "You don't have to tell me this."

Mark placed a finger under her chin and turned her face back to him. "I do. It was an automatic mechanism to protect myself. I only compounded the problem by misreading your reserve. Every time I asked you a personal question, you gave me the cold shoulder."

His need to explain only made things worse. "I've never done that. Talk about getting your signals crossed."

"I thought you were a career woman. Like my ex." Mark took a sip of his drink.

"What gave you that idea?"

"The way you put your whole heart into your job. Until recently I would have bet that you didn't have a life outside of the office."

"It just means that I'm conscientious. And yes, I do have a life outside of work." As rare as it might be, she did socialize. Amanda was annoyed that he could read her so well. "So you finally understand me. That doesn't change the fact that you wanted to keep our relationship business-only. What happened to being just friends?"

"I lied."

Amanda jabbed Mark's chest. "You're driving me crazy! One minute you're acting one way and the next you're heading in the opposite direction."

Mark placed his hand on top of hers, the jolt of his warmth stilling her movements.

"From now on I'll make my messages loud and clear."

"What do you intend to do?" Were her dreams unfolding in front of her very eyes, or was she seeing things that really didn't exist?

"Be there."

That's it? That's all Mark was willing to offer? One minute she was holding her breath, flushed with hope, the next a cold emptiness settled where her heart was. Perhaps he wasn't capable of deeper feelings for her. Amanda placed her glass down and steeled herself for his words.

"Go on."

"I accept that you've made up your mind about your job, but I don't want to lose what we've just discovered."

Her eyes rounded. "Wow." So much honesty. "I thought I was the one afflicted with the spell."

"Maybe it's contagious."

Amanda had difficulty swallowing. "How far do you intend to take this?" she asked, clasping and unclasping her hands.

"As far as you want."

She let her dice and her mouth roll. The way she figured, she had nothing to lose. "I want you to get to know the real Amanda and not compare me to your past regrets." She shifted away from him.

"Agreed."

She needed to think clearly and with Mark so close she couldn't. Amanda wanted to embrace everything he offered. And yet she hesitated. Was it the outspoken Amanda that sat in front of him that he wanted or the gentle woman who existed beneath? Amanda tucked her leg under her and gave Mark a pensive look.

"Ask whatever your heart desires," he encouraged, caressing the side of her face.

Amanda's heart jumped at his feathered touch. He was already there. He'd been there from the day he had taken over the office. Taken over her life. Amanda nervously licked her lips. "Why now? What made you change your mind?"

Mark scratched his head. "Two things. The first was the lingerie. When I thought you had bought it for Tony, I saw red. I wanted it for myself. When you walked out of that laundry room wearing only my shirt, it really hit me what I had lost."

What had he lost? The old, sweet Amanda that still lurked beneath or the new Amanda, with her flamboyant clothes and sassy mouth?

"And the second?" Amanda held her breath.

"Your resignation. When you leave, I'll miss the Amanda I've come to know."

And love?

"I appreciate your honesty, but at the end of the two weeks, I'll be starting my new job. And it won't be because of you, even though it was at first, but because I've realized it's what I want."

"I'll quit if you still want to stay."

Amanda sadly smiled. "That won't be necessary." She couldn't believe that he would give up his job for her. How unfair was life? Mark had given his heart away to his ex and she had used him to get promoted. Now he was willing to leave his job for her, yet he didn't love her. Talk about poetic justice.

"You can't get rid of me that easily."

Still insecure, Amanda needed to think about it. "I won't, but I've been hurt before and I don't intend to let it happen again."

"Who hurt you?"

"I had a boyfriend in college who manipulated me. If I dressed or said anything to displease him, I received verbal abuse that scarred me emotionally. It left me doubting my own self-worth."

Mark leaned away and frowned at her. "Have you ever thought I might be gun-shy because the last woman I went out with said one thing and did another? It's not only women who get burned, you know. I'll admit that I was playing the field, but in actual fact I was playing it safe. Haven't you heard the saying, safety in numbers?"

Amanda relaxed. She could tell from his angry flush that her low opinion of him had insulted him. She smiled gently. "I don't think that saying was meant to be used in that context. But I finally understand what you mean."

"Now we're getting somewhere."

"I'm not holding a gun to your head," Amanda pointed out, not wanting him to feel cornered.

"Far from it," Mark sighed deeply. "You've shown me the things I've been missing. Things that I convinced myself I didn't need."

Amanda took a sip from her margarita and patiently waited as Mark pensively stared at the fire and gathered his thoughts.

"I'm successful in my career but my life is empty. You planning your life got me thinking. If you had the courage to move on, then I was cheating myself." It was time to see if he could learn from his past and change.

Standing up, Mark extended his hand. "I'll make dinner."

Amanda placed her hand in his.

Entering the kitchen, Mark wrapped an apron around his hips and grinned at her. "What do you want?" he asked, grabbing a bag of shrimp from the fridge.

"Marriage." The cursed word slipped through her lips.

His smile vanished, along with his color. The bag of shrimp slipped through his fingers and landed on the floor.

"Oh God, not again," Amanda groaned, picking up the bag and handing it back to him. "It's the spell. Ignore what I just said." She walked around the counter to put some space between them.

"I don't think I can."

Amanda was conscious of Mark studying her every move. "Forget about it," she said, trying to brush her words off. "*I'll* sure try."

Grabbing a bottle of white wine from the fridge, Amanda peeled the seal. "It's not like you aren't used to me saying the craziest things." Amanda jerked one drawer after another to find the corkscrew. "Believe me—if I had the choice, most of the things you've heard would have been left unsaid." She found the corkscrew, stabbed the cork with more force than necessary and tried to twist it open.

"Here," Mark said, taking the bottle out of her hands. "Give me that before you stab yourself." With one smooth tug the cork popped out and he handed the bottle back to her. "Amanda, if you said it that means you meant it."

Amanda poured two glasses and slid Mark's across the counter, raising her own to her mouth and taking a large gulp of courage. "I have no idea where that came from. Everything is settled."

"But the spell?"

"Ha-ha." Her laugh sounded desperate. "You know the spell, just ignore it."

"Ignore it?" Mark banged a skillet on the gas range. "It'd be easier to ignore an elephant in my backyard than the bombs you keep dropping."

"This — you...me...us — shouldn't be, according to the spell." Amanda filled a large pot with water and slammed it onto a burner, spilling water over the edge and making the flames snap and sizzle. "Each time I open my mouth it's like a land mine igniting."

Mark threw chunks of butter and garlic into the skillet. "Forget about the spell and for once do what you want."

"That's exactly what I'm trying to do." Amanda felt an arc of tension jump between them.

The shrimp sizzled, the water boiled, the kitchen filled with heat and the aroma of garlic, while an uneasy silence baked between them.

Their dinner, to put it mildly, was very uncomfortable. Amanda stood up from the table, her food mostly untouched. "I'll wash since you cooked," she said with a smile she didn't feel.

Without saying a word, Mark poured himself another glass of wine and headed outside for some fresh air. What a mess this was. Their timing was totally off.

Amanda filled the sink with soapy water and dropped in the pots to soak. This was just great. When she had wanted a full-steam-ahead relationship, he was at a dead stop. When he'd finally accelerated to catch up to her, she had already taken the next exit route off the highway that was their relationship. And now when he wanted to take things slow, she wanted to put the pedal to the metal.

She didn't want slow. She wanted high-speed, in-your-face, accelerated exhilaration. All her life she'd had safe and slow. No more. She had Mark, here and now, and she wasn't going to let this opportunity slip away. She'd let him take a peek at her chassis and hoped that he liked what he saw so much that he'd want to look under the hood.

Looking out the sliding doors, Amanda spotted Mark with his back to her, staring out at the night. If things were different, Amanda would have joined him or even suggested a swim to get rid of all her tension.

Needing time to think, she quickly cleaned up the kitchen and made herself a cup of herbal tea in the hope that it would relax her, then headed upstairs.

In the bathroom, Amanda stripped then pampered herself with lotion, softening her skin with the vanilla-scented cream. Her body tingled with a rose blush of health. About to slip on the peignoir she had bought, Amanda heard movement coming from Mark's room. Peeking through the crack in the washroom door, she watched Mark take his shaving case out of his bag.

Sneaking back into her room, Amanda quietly closed her door. Once the shower started, she moved away. She clasped her shaking hands together as anticipation and fear ran high.

She quickly donned the cream-colored, sheer peignoir and took deep breaths as she contemplated her next move. She'd show Mark what he was missing and if it didn't work, then at least she'd have something to remember him by. All she had to do was gather her courage and figure out how to use it.

Hands shaking, Amanda smoothed the transparent folds over her body. Every movement made Amanda aware of the energy charging her skin, her pleasure points.

Listening, she realized that the shower had stopped. The coast was clear to grab the tube of amaretto chocolate body paint to add to her seduction. Tiptoeing back into the bathroom, Amanda picked up the body paint and read its label. "I wonder if it tastes good?"

"We could always find out."

From the doorway, Marks deep voice embraced Amanda's heightened senses. That's it? All she'd had to do was wear a transparent nightgown and wave a tube of body paint in her hands to tempt him?

She looked into the mirror and watched him rub a towel across his chest. Her bright green eyes held his tempting blue ones as he entered the bathroom.

Mark devoured her image in the mirror. The cream peignoir sculpted the lush curves of her body. The tiny spaghetti straps clung perilously to her smooth shoulders while the transparent lace design over her swollen breasts hid nothing. The wisps of fabric caressed her hips and settled at her feet. His hungry eyes traveled down her body to rest on the center of her desire.

The room shrank when Mark came to stand behind her. She held onto the counter for support and watched the towel sail into a corner. The mirror exposed their flushed bodies, their darkened eyes. Each short, rapid breath bounced off the enclosed space.

Mark's pajama bottoms sat precariously low on his narrow hips. His powerful build was magnificent compared to her smaller frame.

He took the tube from her hands and squeezed the paste onto one of his fingers. Reaching around her, Mark traced her bottom lip. "How does it taste?"

Her tongue emerged to wet her lips and taste the chocolate. The flavor exploded in her mouth. "Delicious." Her reflection blushed, the tips of her ears burning just thinking about how decadent the rest of her body might taste.

Mark brought his finger to his mouth and slowly sucked the remaining chocolate. "A tasty appetizer."

Amanda's breathing increased when Mark placed the tube on the counter, within easy reach. She bit her lower lip, not knowing what she should do next. She hadn't thought she'd make it this far.

"Relax," Mark said, squeezing her shoulders. "Anything you want, I'll want."

His warmth melted away any final insecurity.

Her heart beat like a trapped little bird. Impatient for more, she turned around in his arms. Mark's soft chest hair was just inches away from her face. It traveled down to a V-shape over his flat stomach. Too tempting to resist, Amanda slowly ran her hand over his chest. His muscles flexed at her touch.

Clasping her hand, Mark blew softly on her wrist then nipped the tender skin at the base of her thumb. Intense blue eyes stared at her. Mark leisurely kissed each finger. Her eyes were wide saucers by the time he reached her pinky. She hadn't known she could experience such pleasure with just kisses to her hand.

Mark guided her hands up his chest, past his shoulders and behind his neck, where he linked her fingers together. He then glided his hands down her arms to wrap them around her waist.

Bending closer, Mark kissed the side of her neck. At the touch of his moist lips against her heated skin, Amanda's heartbeat jumped. His lips against her pulse sent shivers along her spine. Her legs shook with each wicked thing his tongue did. His touch ignited a tingle that intensified with each caress.

"Nervous?" Mark caressed the sides of her body.

"Yes," said Amanda in a husky voice. Her eyes caressed his flushed skin. Amanda was pleased that they were combusting together. Tentatively, Amanda played with the short curls at the back of his neck and watched his eyes dilate.

"I'm glad I'm not the only one."

With a sense of newfound power, Amanda brought her hands down to brush them back and forth over his nipples, enjoying Mark's hiss of pleasure. She inhaled their mingled scents. Encouraged by his reactions, Amanda pulled him closer and brushed her body against his.

Mark moaned. "What do you feel?" he asked, the pulse at the base of his neck racing, his eyes narrowed.

"Breathless. My body's tingling—I ache."

"Show me where."

"Here." Amanda cupped her breasts over her nightgown.

"What else do you feel?" Mark removed her hands and kneaded her breasts, making Amanda press deeper into his touch. He traced the form of her breasts and circled around the nipples. Tightening the caress, he pressed her nipples between his thumbs and fingers. Waves of desire shot from her breasts to her vagina as he rotated the nipples into a hard nubs.

"Fire. A hot, consuming blaze." Amanda groaned when Mark's hands traveled to the base of her stomach. He created electrical ripples of reaction with his hands. "If you don't slow down, I'm going to fall apart."

He brought her body flush with his and let her feel what her honesty did to him. "Lady, by the time I'm finished with you, you're going to scream."

Her turgid nipples rubbed against his chest. Amanda closed her eyes and tilted her head back. She moaned in ecstasy when he pulled her hips tight against his and gyrated.

"Promises, promises." She stood on the tips of her toes to kiss Mark's neck. He smelled of soap and hot passion.

Amanda scattered light kisses from the top of his shoulder down, to circle around his nipples. Her tongue traced the fine hairs that surrounded them. Mark buried his fingers in her hair and pressed her firmly over his unyielding contours.

Biting down on his skin, Amanda enjoyed the growl that vibrated beneath her lips. She needed to see more of him. With trembling hands, she gently cupped his face. "I need more," she said, exposing her need and vulnerability with open honesty.

Without glancing away, Amanda smoothed her hands down to the elastic waistband of his pajamas. Mark sucked in his stomach at her touch. Slowly hooking her fingers, she tugged his bottoms past his arousal, which jutted out proudly, over muscular thighs, and over tension-filled calves to finally pool around his feet. Through hooded eyes, he followed her every move. She understood how difficult it was for him to remain still.

Amanda stood and took a small step back. Mark clenched his fists at his side. He seemed to understand that she needed to be in control. He made no sudden moves, but his stillness cost him greatly. She had undressed him as though she were carefully opening a Christmas present and hadn't wanted to rip the paper.

"You're killing me," Mark said, kicking his pajama bottoms away.

"Likewise." Amanda pulled Mark closer and sucked his bottom lip before opening her mouth to enjoy the aggressive thrust of his tongue.

Mark traced the lines of her body lovingly. Amanda arched her back, pressing deeper into his hands. Heat flared. The possibility of endless delights hardened his throbbing penis as moisture gathered at its tip.

"Damn, you're beautiful," Mark said, cupping her breast over the sheer fabric.

Amanda was a temptress, a tease. His body teetered close to the edge of shattering. His tight restraint kept him in a self-imposed lock. She learned his body, each inquisitive caress gifting him with unbearable pleasure.

"So are you," Amanda returned, smoothing his soft chest hair.

"Now it's your turn," Mark said with a deep, guttural voice.

With an alluring smile, Amanda crossed her arms and lifted the negligee over her head.

Mark threw back his head and moaned. If Amanda didn't move soon, he would snap. Her soft caress on his neck brought his focus back to her.

Amanda pulled his face toward her and nipped at his swollen lips. "Lie down. I want to touch all of you."

Mark felt beads of sweat form on his forehead and upper lip as he obeyed. Amanda knelt beside him. She ran her hands over his sculpted chest and teased past his flat stomach where his fine hair ended.

She traced large circles on Mark's abdomen to his thighs. With each passing circuit, she moved in closer. He held his breath and waited.

Smaller and smaller the inner circle became until her goal was in hand. Instead of giving Mark what he craved, Amanda widened the area all over again and watched him grow harder. It was pure, unadulterated torture.

Stopping only for a second, Amanda reached for the body paint and squeezed it in a zigzag pattern across his chest. She trailed her finger through the paste and brought it to her mouth. "Delicious." Amanda swirled her tongue around her finger.

"You're a witch."

Amanda leaned over and licked her way down to his stomach. She spread the amaretto chocolate, making groves with her nails. Her talented tongue followed, causing his muscles to jump, his blood to surge.

His fists clenched the carpet as the torture continued. Each time Amanda drew closer to his arousal, he tightened his buttocks and raised himself off the carpet. His head was thrown back, his neck muscles taut as he neared his limit.

Finally Amanda wrapped her tiny hands around him, making him jerk. Shivers coursed through his body.

"Like I said—beautiful." Amanda spread the remainder of the paste on his arousal and finally brought him fully into her mouth. Amanda moved her hands up and down and stimulated him further.

At his wit's end, Mark took hold of her wrists to still her hands. "Enough." He wouldn't get the chance to show Amanda how special she was if she continued.

Sitting up, Mark gently pulled Amanda's hands away from him and laid her down with her hands captured above her head. "Now I'll show you how delicious you are."

Taking hold of the tube of body paint, Mark squeezed the paste around each nipple and trailed a line down her stomach to where her curls started. Placing both hands on each side of her head, Mark leaned over and kissed the tops of her breasts, moving up to her swollen lips. He devoured her lips, plunging into her mouth, capturing the taste of amaretto off her tongue.

"You taste unbelievable."

"So do you." Her breathless words ended with a moan.

He continued to torture Amanda in the same fashion she had done. Kissing, nibbling and licking, Mark traveled over her most sensitize areas to her pelvis bone. He blew on her curls, teasing her, before returning to her breasts once more.

Amanda's body moved from side to side. "Please."

"Want me to stop?" asked Mark in a hoarse voice.

"No…yes…I mean…" stuttered Amanda.

"This." He finally gave her what she needed. Mark sucked her nipple deeply into his mouth. He laved one breast before pleasuring the other as Amanda pulled his head closer. He compressed his lips, making shivers course over her body.

She threw her head back, her body vibrating with pleasure. Releasing her nipple, Mark licked his way down to her stomach and stuck his tongue into her navel, making her abdominal muscles convulse.

With hands that shook, Mark spread her thighs open. He smoothed her curls and softly stroked her wetness. Each fold clung lovingly to his fingers, ready for him.

Sensing that Amanda was close to her orgasm, Mark fumbled through his shaving case, retrieved a condom and slipped it on. Holding his weight on his arms, he hovered over her and with a firm thrust, entered.

Stilling, Mark looked into her beautiful eyes and waited for her to adjust to his size. "Okay?"

"Don't stop." She clenched her inner walls around him.

"God, do that again." Mark felt Amanda's insides grip him and he responded with a pulse of his own. Wrapping her legs around his waist, she raised her bottom and joined them deeper.

Picking up her pace, Mark matched each movement to Amanda's. Faster, harder, his breathing quickening. Mark held back so that Amanda could reach her completion first.

"Let yourself go. I'm here," Mark promised.

Amanda emitted a high-pitched scream before he took his pleasure, arching his head back to release a satisfied groan that erupted from his very depths.

Making sure not to put his weight down on her, Mark collapsed on his side, clasping Amanda close to him. As their breathing and heartbeats slowed, Mark caressed her as the final ripples consumed her body. "You are absolutely beautiful. Watching you only increased my pleasure that much more."

"I felt the same thing." Stretching like a satisfied cat, Amanda languidly traced letters with the remaining paint on Mark's chest. "We're a mess."

"That's easily fixed." Mark stood up and lifted Amanda off the carpet.

Amanda squealed. "This paint makes me slippery."

Mark put her back down on her feet and kissed a chocolate smear off her cheek.

He turned the shower on and pulled Amanda in. What started as a relaxing scrub turned into an erotic game. Slowly lathering each other's bodies, they brought each other to orgasm again amidst the steamy heat of the shower.

When they finished, Mark stepped out and wrapped a towel around his hips before toweling Amanda. He sat her down on the side of the tub and blow-dried her hair. He combed his fingers through her hair and watched it dry into bouncy, corkscrew curls.

"I am so tired." Amanda swayed to her feet and looked around the washroom.

"What are you looking for?"

"My nightgown." She found it lying on the floor covered in chocolate stains. Picking it up, Amanda grimaced. "I guess I can't wear this."

"You won't be needing that," Mark said, taking the gown out of her hands. "Jump into bed while I clean up some of this mess." He nudged her toward her bedroom.

By the time Mark turned off the bathroom lights Amanda was sound asleep. He crawled into bed and pulled her against him in a spoon fashion. He brushed a curl off her face. "What am I going to do with you?" With a resigned sigh, Mark drifted off to sleep.

Chapter Fifteen

🔊

Amanda woke to the smell of bacon and Mark's deep breathing on the base of her neck. Her eyes rounded with the realization that the Bassetts had arrived. The desire to scrabble out of bed and pretend that everything was innocent was enormous. She didn't want to be found in bed with her boss. Well, technically, he'd only be her boss for another two weeks.

Biting her lip, she tried to edge out from under the dead weight of Mark's arm and found that she couldn't budge. He'd wrapped his arm around her waist and pulled her against him. It was as though, subconsciously, he'd made sure that she wouldn't leave.

Not wanting to wake him up, Amanda tried to lift his hand off her waist. With a grumble, Mark buried his face deeper into her neck and cupped her breast. "Oh, shit." She slowly extended her leg over the side of the bed and moved the lower part of her body away. With another mutter, Mark wrapped his leg over hers and settled into her pillow with a sigh.

"Oh for Pete's sake." She blew a curl out of her face and peeked behind her to come face-to-face with devilish blue eyes.

"Where do you think you're going?"

"Phil and Donna are downstairs." Glancing at her watch, Amanda saw that it was already after ten o'clock. "Donna will have seen the two vehicles outside and know that I'm not alone. She'll wonder what's keeping us."

"No she won't. She also knows it's me who's up here because she'll recognize my car." Under the covers, his hand roamed over the curve of her hip to caress her bottom.

With a squeak, Amanda slipped off the bed onto the floor. "No way. If we start now we won't show up until lunch." A deep flush burned her cheeks as she lifted herself off the floor.

Mark put his hands behind his head and gave her a smile that sent her pulse racing. "That's fine by me."

Amanda grabbed a pillow off the bed and threw it at him. He easily caught it and placed it behind his head.

Conscious of Mark watching her every move, Amanda gathered her clothes and hurried to the bathroom. "See you downstairs." She stuck out her tongue before closing the door behind her.

Entering the kitchen, Amanda found Phil and Donna already seated at the table. "Good morning. Did you win the regatta?"

"Morning," Donna smiled. "No, we came in second. There's bacon, sausages, eggs and toast in the warmer. Help yourself."

Amanda placed sausages, toast and eggs on a warm plate and sat at the table with them.

"Coffee?" Phil held up the carafe and poured for her. "Is Mark up yet?"

Amanda nearly dropped her cup. "I think he'll be down shortly."

"Darling, sometimes you can be so subtle," Donna said, sending Phil a comically stern look.

"I'm right here," Mark said, entering the kitchen wearing blue jeans, a white T-shirt and open sandals on bare feet. "Good morning." He happily helped himself to the food then sat down beside Amanda. His leg brushed up against hers, making her heart jump.

"What plans do we have for today?" he asked as he munched on his toast.

"I thought I'd pack a picnic lunch and we'd go sailing," Donna answered, sipping her coffee. "We'd be back by early evening, so if we're tired we could take a small nap before dinner. The fresh air and a good workout usually does that to us."

Mark smiled. "Sounds good to me."

The day turned out perfect for sailing. With a cloudless sky overhead and a strong wind at their backs, they skimmed the water at exhilarating speeds from one shore to the next. Their white sails flapped furiously in the wind as the sun reflected off the water and bounced off the shiny chrome railing. People waved to them as they sailed by, or raced them, setting them off with their sails bulging with wind.

At lunchtime they anchored with a group of boats in a sheltered, rocky cove and ate on deck as the boat lulled on quiet waves. Music played, families were introduced as food was passed around. It resembled a party with dinghies being rowed back and forth as everyone shared their food and wine. Children jumped into the water, enjoying the last of the late summer heat.

Throughout the day Amanda caught Mark pensively watching her. An arc of tension and awareness passed between them each time. When Mark wasn't watching her, she would study him. She loved so many aspects of his personality—the way he listened to a grandmother, or how he gently pulled a child away from the railing. His caring showed in his actions.

By late afternoon the party broke up. Hugs and kisses were exchanged before each boat went their own direction.

On the return trip, the sails were lowered so a more leisurely pace could be enjoyed.

Amanda relished the tranquil sounds of waves splashing against the boat's sides as Phil steered. Donna read on the bench beside her and Mark sat at the bow, enjoying the full force of the wind. She wanted to join him but wasn't sure if she should.

As though he sensed her watching, Mark turned around and smiled at her. "Come sit with me." Amanda stood up and maneuvered toward him. When she was beside him he pulled her in between his legs and settled her back against his chest. He wrapped his arms around her and pulled her into him. "Glad you came?"

"Wouldn't have missed it." She knew she glowed from a day on the water. Her cheeks felt pink from the sun and the wind.

He gently wrapped a twisting curl behind her ear that had escaped her clip. "You're amazing," he said, peering down at her with a serious expression.

Amanda wrapped her hands around his arms and savored the closeness. She felt cherished.

Mark cleared his throat. She could feel his body stiffen with tension beneath her hands. "You know after this weekend your aunt is going to want you to make an honest man out of me. Don't you think that we shouldn't upset the dear?"

If he had hit her over the head with a hammer she couldn't have been more surprised. "'Honest man', as in marriage?" Amanda had stopped letting herself hope past this weekend. She found herself unprepared for Mark's proposal.

"Yes," Mark sincerely agreed.

Amanda scowled at Mark. "You want to marry me so that you'll be safe from my aunt?"

"Yes…I mean no." Mark swatted his hair away from his face. "That's not what I meant at all. I'm not doing a good job of it. I want to marry you because you're an amazing woman, you're caring and unselfish."

She knew her good points. "And?" Amanda waited for the answer she needed.

"You have the same ideals as mine. Our family would come first and I know you'd make a wonderful wife and mother. I adore the things you do and the things you say."

Still not enough. "And?" she asked again, elbowing Mark in the stomach. She still hadn't heard the words she needed. "Three strikes and you're out."

"Because I love you!" Mark triumphantly shouted over the wind.

Amanda twisted in his arms, throwing hers around his neck and kissing him with all her heart.

Amanda heard a hoot of triumph. Separating, she found Phil dancing at the helm. "It's about time, my boy!"

"Leave those two sweethearts alone and quit eavesdropping," Donna admonished, wiping a stray tear and giving a weepy smile.

Phil laughed. "I'm not eavesdropping. It's not my fault that the wind carries their voices all the way back here." Not heeding Donna, Phil challenged Mark, "Now pay attention and watch this old sailor to learn how it's done." He hoisted Donna off her feet like a pirate and kissed her.

Amanda laughed at his antics. "I hope we're like them when we get to their age," Amanda laughed, watching Donna and Phil embrace.

"Most likely. Being young doesn't have a monopoly on antics. And speaking of antics, do you want to call your aunt when we get back to the cottage?"

"If I know her, she's been waiting by the phone all weekend while watching her favorite shows." Amanda hugged Mark tightly.

Arriving at the dock, they made quick work of putting the boat in order before heading for the cottage to celebrate. Both couples went their separate ways to shower before meeting again. Using the phone in their room, Amanda called home with Mark sitting beside her on the bed.

Aunt Lilly picked up on the first ring. "What took so long? I was starting to get worried!" Aunt Lilly shouted over the sound of a game show playing in the background.

"Why?" Amanda grinned at Mark as he listened to the conversation.

"What do you mean 'why'?" yelled Aunt Lilly. "Did he or didn't he pop the question? Do I have to come up there and show him how it's done?" They could hear the agitation in her voice.

Amanda put her out of her misery. "He did and we are."

"Hot damn!" Aunt Lilly bellowed over the line. "I knew the boy had it in him."

"Do you want to talk to him?" Amanda asked.

"No, no. Just give him a big kiss from me and tell him he's lucky to be getting you. Enjoy yourselves. Now let me go," ordered Aunt Lilly. "I'm in the middle of one of my shows and I'm doing better at guessing the prices of the items than the bozos on the screen. Bye," she said and hung up.

Amanda put the phone back in its cradle. "Did you hear?"

"All of it." Mark stood up and extended his hand. "Let's hurry, Phil and Donna will be getting things ready. Later we'll have a celebration of our own."

The couples drank champagne and enjoyed a rich meal of fettuccine Alfredo, veal cutlets sautéed with mushrooms in a white wine sauce, and tomato slices with bocconcini drizzled with oregano and olive oil. With the meal completed, the day spent in the sun caught up with Donna and Phil. The couple said their goodnights and Amanda and Mark returned to their room to finish the evening with a celebration of their own.

Together, they lit the scented candles and poured the bubble bath into the Jacuzzi to create a rich foam. Two glasses filled with wine stood beside the half-eaten box of truffles, all within reach. Leisurely, they took off each other's clothes and stepped into the waiting tub filled with scented water and bubbles.

"Come here," Mark said, pulling her in between his legs and settling her back against his chest. "I love you." He caressed the bubbles over her breasts.

Amanda hugged his arms closer to her. "I've waited so long to hear you say that, I'm not going to get tired of you repeating yourself."

Mark caressed the bubbles over her body. "Do you have any other fantasies you want to share with me?"

When she didn't answer, he nudged her with his shoulder to make sure she hadn't fallen asleep on him. "Amanda?"

Her smile turned into a grin as astonished disbelief turned into rapture. "Ask that again."

"I asked if you had a fantasy you wanted to share with me," Mark repeated, perplexed at her demand.

Amanda threw herself against Mark and laughed uproariously.

"What did I say?"

"It's not what you said, but what I *didn't* say. I didn't say what was on my mind." Amanda rained kisses on Mark's face. "I can't believe it, the spell is gone."

"Are you sure?"

Amanda waited to see if any words would tumble out, for the sensation of her mouth running out of control to take over. When nothing happened she laughed. "Go ahead, ask me a question, I dare you." Amanda wiggled on his lap.

"Would you happen to know who sent that email about Greg?"

"I do, but I'm not saying." She grabbed a handful of bubbles and threw them in the air. "This is great, just great! Ask me another."

"Okay, how would you like to play a game of strip poker?"

"Not. Besides we're already naked. Hit me with another one."

"Which of my body parts is your favorite?" Mark shimmied his hips from side to side."

"Talk to the hand," Amanda said, waving it close to his face then running her fingers down his chest. "Or I could make my hands talk for me."

"Not a bad idea."

"I'm free!" Amanda threw more bubbles into the air. "I'm really free."

Mark wiped the suds off his face. "You know I'm going to miss that thing."

Amanda playfully punched him in the stomach. "Have you lost your mind? Do you know what a relief it is? There won't be any more blurting things out to strangers, or making enemies of people. I won't be miserable because I can't keep a secret, or wonder when the next time will be that I step in my own shit."

"I enjoyed your candid moments," he smirked. "Well, most of them."

"I didn't. My body was always in a cold sweat, worrying about being surrounded by people, their eyes zeroing in on me each time my tongue flew out of control."

Mark wrapped her back into his arms. "You'll never have to go through that again. Still, I got to hear some pretty good stuff."

"What if I show you what I'm thinking instead?" She wiggled on his lap.

"I could compromise with that."

Instead of answering, Amanda showed him.

The next day, when they were about to leave, Donna presented Amanda with the painting of the little girl tapping the turtle's shell. A pre-wedding gift.

Tearfully, Amanda hugged Donna. "This is too much."

"Nonsense. Don't forget that I have the original little girl. I even painted yesterday's date in the corner next to my name so you'll always remember when Mark proposed."

Amanda started to cry all over again.

"Now, no more blubbering. If you start, then Donna will follow," Phil said.

"No, I won't," Donna protested, tears gathering in her eyes.

"Off with you," commanded Phil gruffly, "and let us know when the wedding is so we can dust off our dancing shoes." Amanda waved at them as she drove away with

Mark behind in his car. She drove just above the speed limit and made it back to her house in record time.

"Are you ready?" Mark extended his hand to her as she closed her car door.

More than he knew. "Are you?" She pulled him to the front door, opened it and walked in. "We're home," she called.

Aunt Lilly raced to them as fast as her feet could carry her. "I'm so happy for you!" She kissed Amanda on the cheek, then Mark.

"Where's Sarah?" Amanda asked.

"I needed some things so I sent her to the grocery store."

"Again?" Mark asked.

Aunt Lilly winked at him. "But why are we standing in the hallway? Come in, come in." Aunt Lilly took Amanda's bag out of her hands and deposited it on the stairs.

"We can't stay," Mark said, wrapping his arm around Amanda's waist. "We're driving up to my parents' house to break the news to them."

"Not to worry then. When you get back we'll have plenty to talk about." Aunt Lilly hugged them once more and waved them out the door.

Approaching the entrance to the highway, Mark took his hand off the steering wheel and clasped Amanda's. "Are you ready?"

"Yes," she replied. "Thanks for asking."

Why an electronic book?

We live in the Information Age—an exciting time in the history of human civilization, in which technology rules supreme and continues to progress in leaps and bounds every minute of every day. For a multitude of reasons, more and more avid literary fans are opting to purchase e-books instead of paper books. The question from those not yet initiated into the world of electronic reading is simply: *Why?*

1. ***Price.*** An electronic title at Ellora's Cave Publishing and Cerridwen Press runs anywhere from 40% to 75% less than the cover price of the exact same title in paperback format. Why? Basic mathematics and cost. It is less expensive to publish an e-book (no paper and printing, no warehousing and shipping) than it is to publish a paperback, so the savings are passed along to the consumer.

2. ***Space.*** Running out of room in your house for your books? That is one worry you will never have with electronic books. For a low one-time cost, you can purchase a handheld device specifically designed for e-reading. Many e-readers have large, convenient screens for viewing. Better yet, hundreds of titles can be stored within your new library—on a single microchip. There are a variety of e-readers from different manufacturers. You can also read e-books on your PC or laptop computer. (Please note that Ellora's

Cave does not endorse any specific brands. You can check our websites at www.ellorascave.com or www.cerridwenpress.com for information we make available to new consumers.)

3. *Mobility.* Because your new e-library consists of only a microchip within a small, easily transportable e-reader, your entire cache of books can be taken with you wherever you go.

4. ***Personal Viewing Preferences.*** Are the words you are currently reading too small? Too large? Too... ANNOYING? Paperback books cannot be modified according to personal preferences, but e-books can.

5. ***Instant Gratification.*** Is it the middle of the night and all the bookstores near you are closed? Are you tired of waiting days, sometimes weeks, for bookstores to ship the novels you bought? Ellora's Cave Publishing sells instantaneous downloads twenty-four hours a day, seven days a week, every day of the year. Our webstore is never closed. Our e-book delivery system is 100% automated, meaning your order is filled as soon as you pay for it.

Those are a few of the top reasons why electronic books are replacing paperbacks for many avid readers.

As always, Ellora's Cave and Cerridwen Press welcome your questions and comments. We invite you to email us at Comments@ellorascave.com or write to us directly at Ellora's Cave Publishing Inc., 1056 Home Avenue, Akron, OH 44310-3502.

Cerridwen Press
Monthly Newsletter

News
Author Appearances
Book Signings
New Releases
Contests
Author Profiles
Feature Articles

Available online at
www.CerridwenPress.com

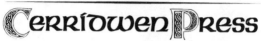

Cerridwen, the Celtic goddess of wisdom, was the muse who brought inspiration to storytellers and those in the creative arts.

Cerridwen Press encompasses the best and most innovative stories in all genres of today's fiction.

Visit our website and discover the newest titles by talented authors who still get inspired—much like the ancient storytellers did...

once upon a time.

www.cerridwenpress.com